The Lion of Yola

S. Ndunguru

Dar es Salam

E & D Limited,
P. O. Box 4460,
Dar es Salaam.
E-mail: ed@africaonline.com

The Lion of Yola
© S. Ndunguru, 2004

ISBN 9987 411 09 6

Cover Illustration: P. Ndunguru

All right reserved. No part of this book may be reproduced in any form without written permission of the publisher.

E & D Limited,
P. O. Box 4460,
Dar es Salaam.
E-mail: ed@africaonline.com

The Lion of Yola
© S. Ndunguru, 2004

ISBN 9987 411 09 6

Cover Illustration: P. Ndunguru

All right reserved. No part of this book may be reproduced in any form without written permission of the publisher.

One

The moon, like a huge luminous sauce pan, rose from a cloudless sky behind a gap in the Livingstone range of mountains to the East of Yola village which lies on the shore of Lake Nyanja. As the mango and the baobab trees dotted over the village began to cast their shadows on the sandy ground, the sound of a drum was heard coming from the direction of Chairman Gaidon Lihimba's home.

Within an hour, the moon had cleared the mountaintops and was smiling serenely over Yola and the adjacent villages. The lake became a silvery expanse and the normally grey sands of the beach glittered in the moonlight. Here and there along the beach, groups of fishermen loaded their nets in small log canoes ready for the overnight routine of fishing. In the meantime, at the sounds of the drum, the teenagers of the village began to converge at Chairman Lihimba's home. Soon the normally sleepy village became alive with song and the throb of drums.

The young folk were celebrating the forthcoming marriage of Lihimba's daughter, Huka, who in a few weeks' time would be marrying Jerome Kawacha, the son of Gabriel Kawacha of the neighbouring Ngumbo village. As was the custom among the Wampoto inhabiting these parts of Lake Nyanja shoreline, forthcoming marriages had to be heralded by nightly *ngoma* dances at the homes of the prospective bride and bridegroom. Young men and women, especially those who belonged to the age group of the future bride and bridegroom would assemble to dance and sing songs, wishing their beloved ones a happy future. Although the songs sung on such occasions usually brought a sense of nostalgia and often drove the future bride to tears, the *ngoma* parties were, on the whole, enjoyed by everybody.

Commencement of the *ngoma* sessions was marked by a formal ceremony performed as soon as all the betrothal formalities had been completed; that's to say, after the young man had paid the bride price to the girl's parents, and the latter had formally given their consent to the impending marriage.

In the case of to-night's *ngoma* the commencement ceremony had been performed the previous afternoon by Mzee Silas Lihimba, elder brother of Gaidon Lihimba. Silas, now in his early seventies, had been *jumbe* of Yola village for twenty years before the system of appointing village chairmen was introduced. Because of old age he had relinquished his duties as the village headman, and the villagers had chosen Gaidon Lihimba as their new leader.

Silas Lihimba's home, on the bank of river Luholochi, was only a mile from Gaidon's home. It consisted of a collection of mud huts for his numerous wives, sons and daughters, and a *boma* for his cattle.

Early that afternoon Silas had left his home accompanied by his eldest wife Chanai; two of his teenage sons, Mika and Luka and his teenage daughter Faith Lihimba. The two boys, leading a fat bearded goat, had led the way, while their sister, Faith, walking behind them, had carried a basketful of cassava flour. Their mother, Chanai, had carried a small basket of fish on her head, and in her right hand she had carried a pair of *manyanga*.

Mzee Silas himself had carried only a walking stick and a small bag made of goatskin.

When the small party of Sila's family approached to within a few metres of Chairman Lihimba's home, Mama Chanai and Faith had simultaneously made a high pitched ululating sound to announce their arrival. This had been taken up by the women folk gathered at the chairman's home. They made similar ululating sounds as they rushed to meet the approaching visitors. Mama Chanai had then intoned a popular song saying, in effect, that she and her husband had come to declare the good tidings that the chairman's daughter had grown up, and that she was ready to go and 'make fire' at Kawacha's home!

The song, with the accompaniment of the *manyanga*, had an immediate impact on the women folk who had rushed forward to meet the visitors. In one chorus they had taken up the song, punctuating their singing with ululation.

After a brief pause during which Silas and his family exchanged greetings with Gaidon Lihimba and his family, the official commencement ceremony had begun. Mzee Silas, accompanied by all the men present had gone outside Lihimba's house. He had taken from his skin bag a small calabash containing a concoction of powdery stuff, and taking a little of the powder, he had cast it in the air on all the four major directions of the earth: north, east, south and west. He had also uttered words to the effect that just as the powder had harmlessly fallen to the ground, he wished that the marriage festivities, which he was inaugurating, would proceed peacefully. He wished that any malice harboured in people's minds to be perpetrated during the marriage festivities would be dropped just as he had dropped that harmless powder. At the end of each incantation those assembled had answered, 'so be it'. Next, Silas had taken from his bag, four small roots which he buried at each corner of Chairman Lihimba's homestead. These spells had been intended to ward off evil spirits who might bring misfortune during the marriage festival. Next, Silas had hoisted a small white flag on the roof of Lihimba's main house.

Now, to every Mpoto tribesman, a white flag hoisted on the roof of a house was the unmistakable sign of an impending marriage. With the hoisting of the flag, the marriage festivities had formally started. From then on there would be nightly *ngoma* dances at Lihimba's home, and relatives would formally begin preparations for the big day. These preparations would include the pounding of corn and cassava for brewing *pombe,* which would be the main intoxicant on the wedding day. The cassava flour would also be used for cooking *ugali* with which to feed the multitudes who would be coming to the wedding feast. The preparations would also include fishing, donation of animals to be slaughtered during the feast; and buying of presents for the bride and bridegroom.

Finally, Silas had slaughtered the goat he had brought and distributed portions of meat to all the relatives assembled. The remainder of the meat had been cooked and consumed by those assembled.

The commencement ceremony had taken place in the afternoon of the previous day. The sound of the drum emanating from Chairman Lihimba's home this evening was summoning the young village folk to their first day of *ngoma*, called *mangaukau*. All the young men stood in a row and about thirty yards away, all the young women stood also in a row, facing the young men. Two boys were furiously beating the drums as the girls wriggled their bellies expertly, and the boys on the opposite side made certain rhythmic movements. Then two boys left their row and advanced towards the girls while making expert dance movements. The nearer they approached the girls' row the more passionate the singing and dancing became. Each of the girls did her best to attract the two approaching young men so that she would be 'picked'. The action of 'picking' a partner, which was popularly known as *kusanga,* meaning to select, was the climax of this dance.

The two boys approached to within a yard of the row of girls and carefully looked round before picking their partners by moving very close to the girl of one's choice and touching her lightly on the shoulder. The two girls thus selected moved forward, dancing behind the returning boys. They in turn would pick two boys of their choice, and so the dance would continue. Although a few odd individuals did take the action of *kusanga* seriously by wishing to establish a permanent friendship with their partners, it was generally accepted that this was only a dance which ought to be enjoyed by all.

The *mangaukau* dance had been going on for some hours and everybody was enjoying himself as the older folks watched the dance without taking an active part in it. All at once the moon was obstructed by what everybody thought was a dark cloud. Everybody looked up at the sky wondering where the cloud had come from since the sky was cloudless that night.

It was at this moment that *Mzee* Susa who had been watching the dance, looking at the thickening cloud exclaimed with emotion, "God of our fathers, locusts! These are red locusts, similar to the ones we had thirty years ago. We have a calamity on our hands.

Stop the *ngoma*. Put out all the lights!"

There was utter silence as everybody gazed at the slowly moving cloud of red locusts. The older folk knew, a calamity was imminent, as Susa had said. If that cloud was to descend upon their village it would mean famine; there would be emaciated bodies and even deaths! But locusts were known to overfly villages and descend on areas remote from human settlements, especially if there was a strong wind to blow them away. The older folk prayed in their hearts that the pestilential cloud would be drifted to far away country. But just then there was only a gentle breeze blowing north-westwards from the south-east.

While the girls and boys dispersed to their homes, the older men remained behind to consult with Chairman Gaidon. It was decided to wake up Bakari Mchope, the local medicineman, whose house was nearby. Accordingly, Susa was dispatched post haste to Mchope's house.

"Open your door, quick!", Susa said knocking on Mchope's door, made of reeds.

"Come out with your medicine kit. We have a calamity on our hands. Locusts!"

"Locusts?"

"Yes, locusts. Don't waste time, you fool!"

"I'm coming. Let me collect my stuff."

After a few minutes Bakari Mchope was standing in Gaidon Lihimba's compound surrounded by the other villagers. He had with him a little black gourd and a flywhisk. He asked for a bowl of water, and then he poured into the water some of the stuff from the black gourd. Dipping the fly whisk into the bowl he sprinkled the liquid in the air, pointing towards the moving swarm of locusts and said,

"You red scourge of mankind,
You insects which bring about famine,
May the wind, aided by this medicine
Blow you to *Ngamanga*,
Where you may perish forever!"

The assembled men answered, "so be it".

Two

The cloud of locusts seemed to have passed on towards the northwest. There was no report of any locusts having been spotted on the ground in Yola village that night. Bakari Mchope was proud of his medicine, and everybody was happy. A calamity had been averted. The village could continue with its merry making in anticipation of the wedding feast of the chairman's daughter.

Early next morning, Huka Lihimba heard a knock on the door of her little dormitory. It was customary among the Wampoto for girls or boys of one age group to sleep in dormitories. There would be several dormitories in a village, some for boys and others for girls; and normally the dormitories were found at the homes of fairly well to do families. Who could be knocking at this early hour of the morning? Huka opened the door only to have a pleasant surprise; for standing outside the house were Jerome Kawacha, her fiancé, and his companion. Unlike on the other visits when such a meeting would have caused smiles, giggles, and jokes, there was seriousness and fear on the faces of the two visitors. Huka welcomed her fiancé and his companion into the dormitory, but Jerome declined to enter saying that they were in a hurry to get back to Ngumbo, and that they should talk where they were.

'What is it that has scared you so?' asked Huka.

'Locusts, my dear. Locusts descended on our village, and we've been sent here to ask for help'.

'Oh, God, why did this happen? Do you know, darling, while we were dancing *mangaukau* last night we saw these locusts flying in the direction of your village. But *Mzee* Bakari, our medicine man, drove them away and we thought they'd never land on our shore'.

'So your medicine man drove the damn things into our village, eh?'

'Oh, no darling. He prayed they'd be blown by the wind to *Ngamanga*.'

'Darling, do you realise what this means to us?'

'It is going to interfere with our wedding'.

'You're quite right. You should see what's happening in Ngumbo. If these cursed insects don't leave, or if they're not destroyed somehow, there isn't going to be a green blade of grass left. This will mean famine; and nobody will be prepared to waste their food stuff over our wedding.'

'Jerome, you realise that we are wasting valuable time?', asked Jerome's companion.

'So you want me to speak to my father right away?', asked Huka.

'Of course, yes. You know I can't talk to him directly. You go and break the news to him. Tell him that my father has sent us here to ask for help. He'll know what kind of help to give.'

Huka left the two visitors and ran to her father's house. She met her father at the door of his house, and before she could break the news, her father told her that he had overhead the conversation between her and the two visitors and that he was already preparing to assemble the villagers. Huka returned to her dormitory and informed Jerome that her father was ready to assemble the villagers.

Shortly after that, the big tom-tom drum was beaten and it was followed by the sound of a horn. It was known by everybody in the village that when the big drum and the horn sounded in the way they did today there was something serious. Only twice in the last twenty years had these signals been given: the first time was twenty years ago when the colonial governor was going to pass through the village; and the second time, ten years ago on the eve of the independence of Kondowe.

The villagers made their way to the assembly *boma* near the primary school: the old and the young, men and women streamed towards the *boma*, for they were sure something serious was afoot. The two couriers from Ngumbo also joined the assembly. As soon as they were gathered inside the *boma*, Chairman Gaidon Lihimba stood up to speak.

'Comrades', he said, 'only an hour ago I beat the ceremonial drum and blew the ceremonial horn. Your response has been wonderful. Within an hour you've all gathered here. This is the spirit; keep it up. And now without wasting valuable time, I'll ask my son-in-law from Ngumbo to break the news to you.'

Jerome Kawacha stood up to address the villagers. After a courteous greeting he went on. 'My fathers, mothers, brothers and sisters; my companion here and I were sent by our elders to ask you to help us fight locusts which last night descended on our village!'

There were frantic screams from the crowd as soon as Jerome had made this opening statement. He went on:

'The whole of Ngumbo village is covered with locusts. There are locusts everywhere: on roof tops, on tree branches, on the ground, in the fields, and even in the lake. Tree branches are broken due to the sheer weight of these insects. Walking along the foot paths is difficult because locusts fly all round you; they strike your eyes, nose and ears. Comrades, unless these insects are destroyed, there won't be a green leaf left in Ngumbo by nightfall. We're asking you to come and help us fight this enemy.'

Old Susa replied, 'We've heard the message, and we understand its meaning. There's no point in wasting any time. We must all start off at once. Any of us who owns a *sau* net, the circular net fixed on a wooden frame, should bring it along, for it is the most efficient implement for catching locusts. Those who have no *sau* net will have to use tree branches to kill the locusts.'

'I'm not going to bring my *sau*' said Bakari, the medicine man. 'I'm going to carry my medicine. What's needed is to cause a strong wind which will make the locusts air borne and eventually carry them away across the lake.'

Chairman Gaidon could not control his anger when he heard Bakari say this. He thundered, 'Stop this nonsense, Bakari! The times when you used to deceive people are gone. Throughout your life you've been collecting goats, cows, money and other things by deceiving people that you could do things which you jolly well knew you couldn't do. Cause a strong wind, indeed! How do you propose to do that? You think we are fools to believe this nonsense? What did you say yesterday? Didn't you say the locusts would be blown away to *Ngamanga?* Is Ngumbo your *Ngamanga?* Comrades, let's start off without delay. Follow Susa's advice. Get your *sau* nets, and forget people like Bakari!'

Bakari Mchope was about to reply when he was interrupted by the sound of the ceremonial horn signifying the end of the meeting. Some people ran to their homes to collect their *sau* nets, and others left immediately for Ngumbo.

The village of Ngumbo was separated from Yola village by the Munyamachi river. Only a kilometre or so after the Yola villagers had crossed the Munyamachi they began to see locusts flying here and there. The farther they moved into Ngumbo village the more numerous the locusts got, until it became almost impossible for them to continue walking. With every step that one made, a cloud of locusts was raised into the air. There were locusts everywhere. It was difficult to see any green leaves. Then, coming from the direction of the village *shambas* could be heard the screams of women and the cries of men as they desperately fought the locusts.

It was about nine o'clock when Jerome Kawacha led the Yola villagers to the *shambas* to join the host villagers in fighting the locusts. Without any preliminaries, the visitors joined in the fight. The best way to fight locusts is to catch them using a round net locally known as *sau*, and throwing them into a fire. Each man with a *sau* was swinging it in the air and catching the locusts. When the net was too heavy to hold in one hand the locusts were emptied into a huge log fire. Those who had no nets, most of the women and some of the men, used only tree branches to kill the locusts, thus causing damage to the crops: cassava, maize, and other plants. The many people milling in the small *shambas* also trampled upon the growing plants. It was a hopeless operation, for, although the locusts were being destroyed, so also were the crops.

By mid afternoon everybody was tired. Lots of locusts had been burnt, and here and there could be seen heaps of locusts killed by the women and children using tree branches. But it was clear that only a fraction of the locusts had been destroyed so far. As the weary people moved about the little *shambas*, small clouds of locusts could still be seen hovering overhead. It was a hopeless battle. Everybody knew that by nightfall there would be no green leaves left in the *shambas*.

The womenfolk who had remained at home to prepare food for the gallant fighters now came to the battlefield bringing food. The exhausted villagers sat down under the shade of trees to take their food. There was little conversation as they ate, for they knew what was going on in the mind of each other. Everyone was thinking ahead of what he'd do when the famine started: visit distant relatives? Sell the family goats and use the money to buy food? Enlarge the family fishnet and do more fishing to make more money?

After the midday meal the battle resumed. But this battle would have to stop by nightfall. It would be impossible to catch the locusts in the moonlight, and the use of light torches would be out of the question for fear of attracting fresh swarms of locusts.

At sunset, just as the men were folding their *sau* nets ready to leave, a wind began to blow from the north. It was gentle at first, but in just under half an hour it became a strong gale. In the meantime Bakari Mchope was standing outside Kawacha's house. He stretched his arms in the air, and facing north from where the wind was blowing he said,

'*Chiwuta*[1], You who created the winds,
Chiwuta, You who created the locusts,
Chiwuta, You who created the herbs
and breathed in them Your own breath,
grant that the herbs may cause the wind to blow,
that the wind may blow the locusts away,
that by blowing the locusts away famine may be averted.
Hear Thou my humble prayer of thanks-giving,
For you have heard my supplication,
You have blessed my herbs,
You have commanded the wind to blow.

Blow on mighty wind and sweep this scourge away!'

The gale became stronger and stronger and a great storm called *mmbelu* arose in the lake. The joy that was felt in every breast was inexplicable. Could this be true? Was this mighty wind going to blow away the deadly insects? People were filled with a sense of expectation as they huddled in their mud houses for fear of the storm outside. The villagers from Yola had to find accommodation in friends' homes as they could not return to Yola during the night because of the storm.

But what had actually happened? What role had Bakari Mchope played? Bakari had been scolded by Chairman Gaidon Lihimba for suggesting that he would cause a strong wind to blow. He had accompanied his fellow villagers to Ngumbo, but instead of carrying his *sau* net and joining the others in the fields, he had proceeded unnoticed, to the mouth of the Munyamachi River. He spent the whole day there invoking the name of *Chiwuta* and immersing in the river certain herbs he had brought with him, so that the juice from the herbs mixed with the waters of the river, which eventually mixed with the waters of the lake. This was the way storm or *mmbelu* was caused according to the belief of the older Wampoto. At the first signs of wind and storm, Bakari left the mouth of the river and hurried to Kawacha's home. It was there that he had said his prayer of thanksgiving.

Early the following morning when the wind had subsided and the lake had calmed, people left their homes and rushed to the fields. Not a single live locust could be seen! It was miraculous. The locusts had indeed been blown away, probably to *Ngamanga*. The heaps of dead locusts, the leafless plants and the ashes of locusts, were all that remained as reminders of what had happened the previous day. As word about Bakari Mchope's activities the previous day began to spread, people hurried to Kawacha's home to have a glimpse of the man who had saved them from the destructive force of the locusts. When they saw Mchope they lifted him shoulder high singing his praises and giving thanks to *Chiwuta*.

Although the locusts had already wrought havoc to Ngumbo village, it was still decided to celebrate in a fitting manner the event of averting what could have been a complete catastrophe. People still hoped that with luck, some of their crops would still regenerate by sprouting new leaf. Plants like rice, groundnuts, cassava, and bananas can grow new leaf even after being visited by locusts, provided they get sufficient moisture. But this was March and the rainy season would be coming to an end in April. There wasn't going to be sufficient moisture to enable the plants to yield a good harvest. The more thoughtful villagers did not go along with the idea of celebrating the event, for they knew that according to their custom, celebrating meant wasting a lot of foodstuff to prepare *pombe*, the local brew. For them it was better to warn the people to be careful with their food and to brace themselves for the hard times ahead. But they dared not voice their objection to the idea of celebrating the big event of the disappearance of the locusts, for fear of incurring the wrath of their fellow villagers.

It was while everybody was congratulating Bakari Mchope that a courier was seen hurrying into Kawacha's compound. It was Mika Lihimba, the son of Silas Lihimba from Yola village. He did not stop to greet the people he met in the compound, but simply shouted,

'Locusts! Our village is covered with locusts! Locusts 've been raining onto our village throughout the night. There isn't a green leaf to be seen in Yola!'

So that strong gale from the north and the great *mmbelu* in the lake had only helped to scoop the locusts from Ngumbo and transport them to Yola! There was a stampede as the Yola villagers started to leave, and Ngumbo villagers followed immediately.

The scene in Yola was exactly like that of Ngumbo the previous day: some people were swinging their *sau* nets to catch the locusts and throw them into the fire, and others were killing the locusts using tree branches. The difference between Ngumbo and Yola villages, however, was that Ngumbo being almost twice as big as Yola, had a total cultivated area which was proportionately larger than that of Yola. Therefore the sudden influx of throngs of people in the tiny *shambas* of Yola and the use of tree branches to kill the locusts did more harm to the crops than was done to those in Ngumbo. By evening there was literally no green blade of grass to be seen in the *shambas*.

Bakari Mchope spent the whole day at the mouth of river Luholochi invoking the name of *Chiwuta* and mixing his herbs with the waters of the river and the lake. But nothing happened: no wind, no *mmbelu*.

By daybreak the following morning the villagers were back in the fields to continue their desperate battle against the vermin. It was a useless fight, for by now the green plants in the fields had virtually disappeared. Some of the villagers sought out Bakari and summoned him before the village government which consisted of Chairman Lihimba and a few elders.

'What's the meaning of this, Mchope?' asked Susa.

'This what?' retorted Mchope.

'This treachery of yours. Why did you cause wind in order to transport the locusts from Ngumbo to our village? See now what they've done. You'll have to pay for it!'

'Don't be over hasty in judging him', intervened the chairman. 'Tell us honestly. Mchope, did you purposely send these locusts here?'

'Mr. Chairman, comrades', answered Mchope, 'I honestly do not understand what you're talking about. Yesterday you, Mr. Chairman, said that I've been deceiving people throughout my life by pretending to do things which, in your opinion, I'm incapable of doing. Today it appears, you've changed your mind and now believe I can cause wind and *mmbelu*'.

'The chairman may have doubted your powers', said Susa, 'but I've always believed that you've these strange powers. That's why I woke you up the other day and asked you to blow away the locusts. I also believe that it was you who caused the gale, which blew the vermin this way. But did you do it on purpose?'

'I swear before you all here, and if what I'm saying now is untrue may I be struck down by lightning, that I had no intention of sending locusts here. Why should I do this? Do I want to see emaciated bodies, and walking skeletons? Do I want to see deaths? What's my profession? Is it not healing people and averting calamities? Have my own *shambas* been spared? No, they've been devastated like all the rest. Yes, I do believe in the potency of the herbs bequeathed to me by my father. But there's more to what I do than the mere use of herbs. I believe in *Chiwuta*. I believe in his powers. He is the one who commands the winds to blow, and *mmbelu* to rise. When I, by the powers of *Chiwuta* and through the medium of herbs, caused the mighty wind yesterday I hoped that the locusts would be blown to *Ngamanga*. I was horrified, as you were, to learn that the vermin had been deposited in our village!'

'Enough of that', said Chairman Lihimba, 'I personally agree with you that you were not responsible for sending the locusts here.

As a matter of fact, I do not believe in the whole business of causing wind and storm by means of herbs. Whatever may have happened yesterday must 've been pure coincidence. You mixed your herbs with the waters of the river and the lake, and you prayed to *Chiwuta*, and by coincidence *mmbelu* started on the same day. That's all there was to it. I really did not see any reason for summoning you here, but since the others demanded that you be brought here, I could not object'.

'Ah, Mr. Chairman!', responded Susa, 'that's your opinion, and of course you're entitled to your opinion. But I do not agree with you; for, I believe that people with special powers and by using special herbs can cause rain, wind and storm. It's not hard to explain these things; for if you believe in an omnipotent *Chiwuta* then there is no reason why he should not be able to accomplish these things through the medium of those he chooses. No, as far as I'm concerned, Bakari Mchope can even now rid us of this menace. This is why we've summoned him here. We want him to do all in his power to rid us of the red plague'.

'I understand your beliefs, Susa', said the Chairman, 'though if we were to hold a serious debate on the question of *Chiwuta's* powers I'd tell you that he does not exercise his powers in an arbitrary manner. He has established laws by which wind, storm, heat, cold, rain, and so on are caused. However it's not my intention to go into all this now. I suggest we all return to the fields and continue our fight against this menace'.

'No, I still feel Bakari should do something', persisted Susa.

'But I've been labouring the whole day long and nothing's happened', complained Bakari Mchope.

'If you were able to help Ngumbo village, you surely must be able to help your own village?', Susa observed.

'It's not a question of choosing whether to help this or that village. It's simply that *Chiwuta* hasn't listened to my prayers, and I think I know why he hasn't answered them. It's because many of you in this village lack faith. Lack of faith prevents my prayers from reaching *Chiwuta*, and there's nothing I can do about it. However, I'll return to the mouth of the river and continue with my ritual. But in the meantime if you're really seriously seeking *Chiwuta's* intervention you must make offering to him. This is what you must do: slaughter a three-year-old ewe and pour its blood as a libation in the river Luholochi. You must burn the meat completely and sprinkle the ashes of the burnt offering in the fields. Do this immediately. I have a feeling that by tomorrow morning the red plague will have left our village. In the meantime I'll continue with my ritual at the mouth of the river'.

Bakari's words were received with applause mixed with reverence. Susa offered to donate his three-year-old ewe, and without delay, Bakari's instructions were carried out to the letter.

By nightfall everybody was exhausted. It was not possible to continue fighting the locusts in the fields, so everybody went home. Only the few elders who had held council with Bakari knew about the offering they'd made to *Chiwuta*. The blood of the sacrificial ewe had been poured into the Luholochi river secretly, and the ashes of the burnt offering had been sprinkled in the fields . There was no wind that night, to the great disappointment of the elders who were expecting a gale and *mmbelu* to start anytime during the night.

Early the following morning everybody left their houses to continue the battle in the fields. To the surprise of all, not a locust could be seen flying. What'd happened? Where were the locusts? The stronger men and the boys began to run towards the *shamba* plots. They reached the fields, but there wasn't a live locust anywhere.

The only signs that locusts had ever visited the village were the leafless plants, the dead locusts on the ground, and the trampled and broken twigs.

'They've left!' Shouted a young man.

'Yes, they've left!' Answered several people together.

'Let's go back and inform the Chairman.'

'Not so hastily. Let's first look everywhere to make sure we're right.'

They searched everywhere: by the riverbank; by the banana groves; in the nearby thicket. They shook trees and combed the bush, but not a single live locust could bee seen. The red plague had indeed mysteriously disappeared! The joy in the villager's faces could not be hidden. Young men hugged one another, and the women-folk that arrived in the fields after the men, made ululating noises, a sign that an enemy has been vanquished.

They all jubilantly returned to the village and surged into the assembly *boma*. Chairman Lihimba and the elders were there to meet the villagers. The Chairman began by thanking everybody for the spirit shown in fighting a common enemy. He had a special word of thanks for the people from Ngumbo and other neighbouring villages. He went on to say that when all hope had vanished, Bakari Mchope, the medicine man, had saved the day. He then narrated to the villagers all that had transpired the previous afternoon. The mysterious disappearance of the locusts, he said, had to be attributed to *Chiwuta's* intervention through his servant Mchope. He urged the villagers to give thanks to *Chiwuta*. He also suggested that some thought be given to awarding Bakari Mchope in a fitting manner.

However, the chairman noted that the red locusts had already caused irreparable damage to the crops. There was hardly a blade of green grass left. This was the end of March and the rains would be stopping in a month's time. It was too much to expect the plants to regenerate sufficiently to give a satisfactory harvest. With a bit of luck the cassava might grow new leaf and the banana plants might grow new shoots. But it was clear there was going to be no rice, millet, maize, beans, and groundnuts. There was, therefore, going to be famine. For this reason the chairman forbade any celebrations being held on account of the disappearance of the locusts and he announced that his daughter's wedding would be celebrated quietly without any feasting. He urged the villagers to buy food from distant villages and stock it; and also to be extremely careful with food. He further suggested that from now on, nobody should be allowed to brew *pombe*.

The Chairman's speech was greeted with mixed feelings. Some thought it was necessary to mark this occasion with at least a few pots of *pombe*, while others thought the chairman had spoken wisely. Finally, however, they all agreed to follow the chairman's advice. They also agreed to donate foodstuffs to Bakari Mchope in appreciation for the service he had rendered.

---

[1] *Chiwuta* means God in the Kimpoto vernacular

Three

As Chairman Lihimba had predicted, there was no harvest to speak of in Yola and Ngumbo during June and July. The hard times predicted by the chairman were indeed approaching. The villagers braced themselves by thoroughly mending their fishnets. From morning to evening and from sun set to daybreak, groups of men took turns in casting their nets in the lake. The fish caught was carefully dried and tied in bundles, and each day a few young men were dispatched to distant villages to exchange the fish for foodstuffs like maize, rice, cassava, millet and potatoes.

This went on for some months, but by September of the same year it was obvious that they were not getting enough food for everybody. The next rainy season would begin in December, and only then would they begin to plant their fields. The next harvest would be in June and July of the following year.

The effects of famine began to show first in the faces of children. No longer could one hear their chatter and laughter. Instead hordes of hungry children could be seen scavenging for food. When the rains started in December school children stopped going to school because their parents bade them to accompany their mothers in search of wild fruits, roots, and mushrooms. Sometimes the mushrooms caused death to a number of people when poisonous species were eaten. Domestic animals were slaughtered and eaten: at first only hens and goats were killed; later, cattle were slaughtered, and much later, some dogs disappeared mysteriously.

The famine continued unabated. Everywhere in Yola and Ngumbo and to some extent in the adjacent villages also, one could see children and grown ups with emaciated bodies. A few individuals were no more than walking skeletons. The time was not far off when people would begin dying.

In March, exactly a year after the red plague had descended on the villages, the new crops were not yet ready for harvest. Unless something was done urgently to bring supplies to the hungry villagers, many of them would succumb to death.

Chairman Lihimba summoned the village government and all the elders of Yola toreview the situation and explore all possible ways of combating their present enemy – famine. Finally it was resolved that a letter jointly written by Yola and Ngumbo residents be sent to Mr. Shedrick Yalomba, Member of Parliament for Lusuma constituency. Mr. Yalomba who was a junior Minister in the Ministry of Economic and Public Affairs had, since his promotion a year ago to this high office, moved into a government house in the Kabisela beach area of Lilungu, the capital of the Republic of Kondowe. Now, partly due to the demand of his high office, and partly due to his contentment with life in Lilungu, Mr. Yalomba had found no time to visit his constituents in Unyanja.

The letter was duly written, and a man was dispatched to Lusuma to post it. It was as thorough as it could possibly be, for it described how the red locusts had descended on the villages the previous year, and how the villagers had fought them. It described the efforts the villagers had made to combat the famine, and it ended by appealing to the MP to seek government assistance for them for the remaining three months while they were waiting for the harvest. It was a touching letter particularly where it gave a graphic description of the ravages of hunger as experienced by the villagers. The letter was signed by Chairman Lihimba and Mahinya, the Chairman of Ngumbo, for and on behalf of the villagers.

It took two weeks for Mr. Yalomba's reply to reach the village chairmen. In his reply the Hon. Shedrick Yalomba promised that he would see the Minister for Provincial Affairs who would attend to the problem of sending relief to the suffering villagers. He went on, in a most persuasive, if rambling manner, to remind his constituents of the central tenet of the Kondowe People's Party (KPP) which was 'resourcefulness in times of difficulty'. He urged them to be resourceful and not to despair. He ended his rambling letter with a string of political slogans, 'Long live the KPP! Long live the doctrine of resourcefulness!'

By the end of May no provisions had been sent to the villages, and of course, Mr. Yalomba had not made an appearance. The affected villagers decided to send a joint delegation to the Provincial Governor whose headquarters were at Lusuma.

The governor listened to the villagers sympathetically, and without delay he ordered the Provincial Agricultural Officer to visit the affected villages and make an on-the-spot assessment of the situation. He was instructed to prepare a full report which would show the extent of the famine, that's to say, the exact number of households affected, the financial position of the villagers, the state of the road leading to the villages, and so on.

It took the Provincial Agricultural Officer two weeks to complete the field assessment and write his report. The report had to be submitted to the Minister for Provincial Affairs in Lilungu; for, according to the highly centralised system of the Republic of Kondowe, the provincial authorities could not do anything without first referring it to the relevant Ministers in Lilungu. So, the Provincial Governor sent the agricultural officer's report to Mr. Henry Kinyua, the Minister for Provincial Affairs, with a covering letter in which he stressed the importance of taking quick action to help the villagers.

Government machinery works slowly. The Minister for Provincial Affairs had to consult his advisors in the Ministry to tell him whether to regard the situation described in the report from Lusuma as an emergency situation or not. Some bureaucrats thought that since only two villages were affected, this could not be regarded as an emergency situation calling for government action at national level. Others advised that the KPP branches of the neighbouring villages should be urged to do something to help their neighbours. Wasn't this what the party meant by resourcefulness in the face of difficulties? A few advisors thought that the situation warranted full government action. They argued that since human lives were at stake, the question whether two villages or ten villages were involved was irrelevant. The matter deserved the full weight of government action. Yet other bureaucrats thought the matter should be discussed at a cabinet meeting! In the end, better counsels prevailed and it was decided that the Minister should visit Lusuma, and from there go on a tour of the affected villages to see for himself whether what the report had said was true.

Among the people accompanying the Minister on his tour of the famine stricken villages of Unyanja was the Hon. Shedrick Yalomba from the Ministry of Economic and Public Affairs. The Lusuma Provincial Governor, the Provincial Agricultural Officer, and the KPP Provincial Chairman were also among the Minister's entourage.

The Minister's party arrived in Yola village on Saturday afternoon. Both Chairman Lihimba and Chairman Mahinya had been informed in advance of the Minister's arrival, and arrangements had been made for the residents of both villages to assemble at Yola to hold a big *baraza* which would be presided over by the Minister.

At 2.00 p.m. sharp three government landrovers pulled to a stop outside the assembly *boma*. The villagers were crowding outside the *boma*. Hungry as they were, they managed to display signs of jubilation by clapping their hands and singing the popular song used at political rallies, '*Pamberi na KPP*', forward with KPP. From the first landrover, which had the word 'POLICE' written on its sides in exceptionally large letters alighted six policemen in uniform. These were, no doubt, the Minister's bodyguards. From the second vehicle alighted the Hon. Shedrick Yalomba, Mr. Malekano, the provincial KPP chairman, and one or two other dignitaries. From the third landrover which was displaying the Kondowe national flag, alighted the Hon. Minister for Provincial Affairs, the Provincial Governor and the Minister's private secretary.

This was a great day for Yola village. Had these distinguished guests visited the village in better times they'd have experienced the hospitality of these simple village folk. They'd have been treated to mountains of rice and *ugali,* and large pots of bubbling *pombe*. But as it was, the guests had to be satisfied with the air they breathed, for the villagers had nothing to offer.

The Hon. Shedrick Yalomba, dressed in a brightly coloured *kitenge* shirt with the picture of the rising sun, the KPP emblem, displayed on the front and back side, promptly began introducing the Minister to the village elders. Mr. Yalomba came from these parts of Unyanja and as a matter of fact, his own village was only thirty odd miles to the south of Yola. He therefore knew the people of Yola and Ngumbo well enough to make flawless introductions. He clearly remembered most of the faces he was seeing since only the year before, which had been en election year, he had been trotting up and down these villages in search of votes. He now picked his way among the milling peasants shaking hands with everybody and introducing the Hon. Minister: "This is *mzee* Susa, a famous fisherman in this village, and member of the village Executive Committee; and, *wazee,* this is our Minister for Provincial Affairs, Mr. Henry Kinyua…. This is the village chairman, Mr. Gaidon Lihimba…, and, oh, this is the chairman of the next village, Mr. Mahinya…. This is Mr. Josaphat, the village school teacher… and this is *Mzee* Mchope, a famous medicine man in these parts…'

As the Minister was shaking hands and chatting with some of the villagers Mr. Yalomba took time to whisper to Chairman Lihimba:

'Did you get my letter, Mr. Chairman?'

'Oh, yes, we did. But why didn't you do something for us?'

'Don't you see I've brought the Minister concerned? I said in my letter I'd inform the relevant Minister. That's precisely what I did; and here he is to-day.'

'But we did not ask you to bring the Minister here. We asked for government assistance. We asked for food!'

'Well, wait and see. The Minister will bring you food. He must first assess the situation, you know. That's how government works.'

'He must assess the situation again? But somebody came here to assess the situation. We thought the next thing we would see would be food. Instead we've more people to assess the situation!'

'You know Mr. Lihimba, government machinery works slowly.'

'Even in emergencies?'

'Well, we don't regard this as an emergency.'

'What? Can you say that again?'

'Don't let us say more about this.'

'By the way, Yalomba, did you really tell the Minister about our letter? Be honest.'

'Of course, I did. How else do you think he could have known about your plight?'

'Alright, I'll ask the Minister himself about it. I've some doubts. Had you told him about us when you got our letter, it is most likely that he would have visited us much earlier. I suspect he must have learned of our problems only after we had seen the Provincial Governor!'

'Oh, so you saw the Provincial Governor?'

'We don't need to go into that now. I'll find out the truth from the Minister.'

The Hon. Shedrick Yalomba did not like Lihimba's attitude just now for it was clear that Lihimba had sensed something and he was in a pugnacious mood. Shedrick knew in his heart that he hadn't done a thing to help the cause of the villagers. He knew that Lihimba was about to find out the truth, and most probably expose it to the constituents. This was going to be disastrous to Yalomba's political career. But there was nothing he could do to save the situation just now, since the Minister had, by now, joined Chairman Lihimba ready to enter the *boma* and begin the *baraza*.

Chairman Lihimba signalled to the villagers to enter the *boma* and get seated orderly. Finaly he led the guests to the dais inside the *boma* and showed them their seats. The six policemen positioned themselves at strategic points inside and outside the *boma*.

The *baraza* started promptly. Gaidon Lihimba thanked the Minister for Provincial Affairs and the Provincial Governor for their visit to the village. He quickly went through the whole story of their plight from the day the red locusts descended on the villages to the present day. He noted that it had taken over two months for the government to begin considering doing something for the villagers. The villagers' letter to their Member of Parliament had been written at the end of March, and this was the beginning of June. He stressed that what the villagers needed now was only enough food to last them the following two months during which they would be gathering their new crops in the barns.

When the Minister for Provincial Affairs stood up to reply to the Chairman's speech he wondered why information about the famine had been kept from him until so late. The first time he had heard anything about the famine had been two weeks ago when he had read the report sent to him by the Provincial Governor. As soon as he had read that report he had initiated top level consultations on the matter, which had culminated in his coming to assess the situation.

Chairman Lihimba could not retain his anger when he heard this. He was shaking all over. He stood up and said,

'Excuse me, Honourable Minister, but only a minute ago I was talking with our M.P. outside there, and he told me that he informed you about our plight as soon as he had received our letter in March! I've a feeling that our M.P. is not telling the truth. He never said anything to you about our problem!'

It was the most embarrassing moment for Mr. Yalomba as the Hon. Henry Kinyua looked at him, and as the villagers began to boo. Gaidon Lihimba went on, 'Comrades, we've been betrayed by our own son. Only last year we gave him our votes hoping that he was going to be an asset to us. To-day he has forgotten us. He has belittled our problem. As a matter of fact, he told me outside there that he did not think that ours was an emergency situation! Comrades, what'd you think about such a man?'

The villagers roared, 'We don't want him. He's no longer our M.P.!'

As the crowd became more and more unruly one of the policemen became nervous and started fingering his belt on which was suspended a pistol, but the Hon. Minister had seen him in time, and he motioned to him to leave the pistol alone. One of the villagers, however, had also seen him touching the belt in the region of the gun. He shouted, 'What's the meaning of threatening us with guns? Kill us, if you want to. It's better to die a sudden painless death at the shot of a gun than to die a slow lingering death due to hunger! We've asked the government to bring us food. But instead you bring us people with guns!'

Chairman Lihimba motioned to the villagers to be quiet. He scolded the young man who had spoken so rashly about the guns, and apologized to the Minister on behalf of the villagers. He also jokingly told the Minister that hungry people were the most difficult people to deal with.

After order had been restored, the Minister ordered the Provincial Governor to make immediate arrangements to bring food to Yola, Ngumbo and those neighbouring villages which had been affected by having had to share their food with the Yola and Ngumbo residents. As there were enough supplies of dried cassava and millet in the godowns at Lusuma these should be distributed free to the villagers. The more expensive food like rice, maize and sugar, which would have to be brought to Lusuma from Lilungu, should be sold to the villagers at reduced price. One bag of maize should be sold for seventy-five shillings instead of one hundred and fifty shillings; a kilo of rice for three shillings instead of seven shillings; and a kilo of sugar for two shillings instead of five. It was up to the village governments to ensure that the free food was distributed fairly among the villagers, and that every villager had the chance of buying the food he needed, if he could afford to. The Provincial Governor promised that the first consignment of free food would be coming in three days' time.

The *baraza* ended happily for everybody except for Mr. Shedrick Yalomba. Outside the assembly *boma* some of the villagers continued booing Mr. Yalomba until his landrover disappeared in the distance.

Four

The first consignment of free food arrived three days after the departure of the Minister for Provincial Affairs. Two lorries one full of bags of dried cassava, and the other full of bags of millet arrived at Yola. The food was to be shared proportionately between Yola, Ngumbo and a few other villages.

Chairman Lihimba made elaborate arrangements to ensure that the food was distributed fairly among the village households. A full list of all the heads of families had been drawn up, and against each name a figure had been written indicating the size of each household. The food was distributed at a specified time under the close supervision of Mr. Lihimba himself. Once a family had received its share, a tick was placed against the name of the head of that family in order to ensure that no family received more than its fair share for one occasion. Any food left over was carefully stored at the chairman's house to be distributed on future occasions, and a careful record of the amount was kept. The same scrupulous handling of the foodstuff could not be attributed to Ngumbo and the other villages. It was rumoured, for instance, that Chairman Mahinya of Ngumbo and his close relatives got exceptionally large quantities of food!

It took two weeks for the more expensive food supplies of maize, rice and sugar to be moved from Lilungu to Lusuma, where it was to be stored, and from there to be sent to the famine stricken villages. The foodstuff was to be sold at reduced price not only to Yola and Ngumbo villages, but also to other neighbouring villages. In all, seven villages were on the list of relief beneficiaries. The chairman of each village was to be responsible for the fair distribution of the free food, and also for the collection of the money paid for the other foodstuff, and for the remittance to government of the cash collected.

It was, moreover, left to the Provincial Governor at Lusuma to make his own arrangements of transporting the food to the villages, for the lorries from Lilungu could not go beyond Lusuma on account of their size and of the condition of the road. The lorries from Lilungu were all seven tonners, and it was not possible for seven tonners to negotiate the dangerous corners in the road connecting Lusuma and the lake shore areas. As a matter of fact, the dirt road from Lusuma to Yola, Ngumbo and beyond was passable for only six months of the year. During the rainy season, November to April, it was so muddy and so slippery that to attempt to drive a lorry on it was suicidal. As most of the bridges on this road were made of wooden poles, sticks and bamboo, it was a common annual occurrence for some of them to be washed away by the torrential rain. This was June, and the rains had stopped in April, but they had left deep furrows on the road, and some of the bridges badly needed mending.

One of the major problems of provincial administration in Kondowe was lack of motor vehicles. It was not uncommon for a provincial headquarters to own less than ten vehicles. The

Provincial Governor at Lusuma had only twelve vehicles, for all the government deaprtments, and these included landrovers and saloon cars. There were only four government-owned lorries, two of which were permanently out of order. Of the remaining two, none of them could be driven on the road to the lakeshore. So when the question of moving food supplies to the famine stricken villages came up, all the Provincial Governor could do was to call a meeting of all the private transporters in Lusuma and persuade them to provide the service.

Only two transporters, Mr. Mchakamchaka and Gulamali Mamdali, offered to do the job. Mchakamchaka was a native of Namatui village on the shore of Lake Nyanja, about twelve miles to the south of the famine area. He was famous in the whole of Unyanja because he was the owner of the Mchakamchaka bus, popularly known as t*he service of the lowly*, which provided the only passenger service to the whole Unyanja. Now with the proceeds which had accrued from his bus service, he had acquired a five-ton second hand lorry. He offered to bring his lorry to Lusuma and begin moving the food to the famine-stricken area.

When the Provincial Governor convened the meeting of transporters, Mchakamchaka was in Lusuma on his regular weekly visits from Namatui. It had taken him three days to travel from Namatui to Lusuma, since he had spent much time on the way fixing some of the broken bridges and, of course, slowly negotiating the badly furrowed road. Also at Msamala village on the way, where his daugther Amelia was married, he had spent a whole day.

The other transporter, Mr. Gulamali Mamdali, was a longtime resident of Lusuma and a famous businessman who owned a fleet of heavy-duty vehicles, including oil tankers. Gulamali had started life as a shop assistant in one of the many shops belonging to Mr.

Manjit, a famous business tycoon in Lilungu. As fate would have it, Mr. Manjit was imprisoned five years ago, on account of a case involving the disappearance of two cases of expensive Rolex wrist watches from the Lilungu Harbours Corporation headquarters. Not only had Manjit been imprisoned, but many of his shops had been closed, and some of his property confiscated by government. It was at this time that Gulamali helped himself to a considerable amount of money belonging to his imprisoned boss, and he had subsequently moved up country to set up his booming transport business at Lusuma.

The task of moving the food began in earnest. Mchakamchaka's old lorry fully loaded with bags of food could be seen labouring down the dangerous slopes of the Livingstone mountains. Mathias Nyoka, nephew of Mr. Mchakamchaka, was the lorry driver. He had been duly instructed by his uncle to make sure that he passed through Msamala village during the night so he could drop a bag or two of maize, rice or sugar at Amelia's house!

When the foodstuff reached the villages, it was off loaded and piled at the Chairmen's homes from where the villagers either collected their rations of free food or bought the other foodstuff. Unfortunately, very few villagers could afford to buy the maize, rice and sugar even at the give away price. Apart from the fact that the fishermen living in this area were generally poor, there being no important cash crop in the area, most of them had already spent their meagre savings to buy food during the year. As a result, most of the food supplies remained unbought, and mountains of bags piled up at the Chairmen's homes.

Gulamali Mamdali saw his chance of making money. The villagers, while queuing to receive their free rations of *makopa* and millet, were simply not buying the other foodstuff.

One evening, Mamdali had just off loaded several bags of *makopa* and millet at the home of Mahinya, the chairman of Ngumbo village, and his turnboy was preparing to begin off loading the bags of rice and maize, when Mamdali decided to engage the chairman in a conversation.

'How's the food situation, Mr. Chairman?'

'Well, it's alright. We're grateful to the government. At least our people are now having something to eat.'

'But why is it that the bags of rice and maize are still piled up in your backyard? Don't they like rice and maize?'

'Of course they do. We're great rice and maize eaters. But we just can't afford to buy the foodstuff. We have no money.'

'What're you going to do about it? Does the government know?'

'Of course the government knows we're poor. But we don't want to complain to government just now since the government has been so generous to us. We're thinking of asking the governor to allow us to distribute the food to our people on credit terms, so that we can pay back slowly within a year or two.'

'I see. But how about yourself, have you got enough for your family?'

'Not at all. Last week I bought two kilos of rice, and that was all I could afford. I've a family of twelve; so the two kilos lasted only one week.'

'One week! How could two kilos of rice, for twelve people, last a whole week?'

'Not twelve, seventeen! The twelve people I mentioned are only my children. When you add my wife and myself and three dependents that are my late brother's children, you get seventeen. Yes, I've to feed seventeen mouths. You see, we don't cook the rice as rice, but we prepare *uji* out of it. What you need is only a little amount of rice and you add a lot of water to it.'

'I sympathise with you Mr. Chairman. Look here, I can give you two bags of rice of my own as a present. But you do me a favour. I'll give you money for all the maize, rice and sugar which I've brought to-day, and you remit the money to the government, and I return with the bags of food. You see, nobody's going to check whether the food was actually bought by the villagers or not. What the government is interested in is to get the money.'

'But won't they find out?'

'Who?'

'The government?'

'Of course not. So long as you've that mountain of bags in your back yard the villagers can't find out that some bags have been taken away by me. Use your brains, Mr. Chairman.'

'I see what you mean. But please see to it that people don't see you returning with the bags of food.'

'Don't you worry about that. Leave that to me. Look at my lorry; when it's locked how can anybody see what's inside it? But on your part, make sure you remit to government all the money I give you. Don't keep a cent for yourself. You see, the exact number of bags issued to me is known and so the government will expect to get the exact amount of money for the bags.'

'I understand that.'

'Good.'

And so after this scheming, Mamdali who had worked out the exact amount of money for the foodstuff he had brought, produced a huge stack of hundred shilling notes and handed it over to Chairman Mahinya.

Mamdali's lorry was one of these modern ones with completely covered iron bodies. So the problem of anybody detecting what kind of cargo was in it did not arise, especially if the journey was made during the night.

Sure enough, Mamdali waited for nightfall; and bidding farewell to Chairman Mahinya, his newly found friend, he started off for Lusuma where he arrival in the small hours of the following day. With his bags of foodstuff which would fetch three times the price at which he had bought them safely in his godown, he settled down to breakfast before proceeding to the Provincial Governor's office to collect his pay for the trip he had just made to the famine stricken area!

Mr. Mchakamchaka, through the activities of his nephew Mathias Nyoka, was satisfied with dropping a bag or two of rice, maize or sugar at his daughter's home, for which he paid at the reduced price through one of the village chairmen. Mamdali thought of extending his influence among the other Chairmen of the famine stricken villages. If ever there was a lucrative business, this was it! Mamdali reckoned that given two months of this business he would be able to fill his huge godown with cheaply obtained food, and later in the year he would resell it at three times the amount of money he had spent buying it. In the black market he could easily sell it at four to five times the price! These were Mamdali's great expectations. He wished, to God, that more villages had been visited by the red locusts!

In the third week of operation, Mamdali decided to send his cargo to Yola village. He had never been there before, since according to agreement between him and Mchakamchaka, he was to begin serving Ngumbo and the villages to the North, while Mchakamchaka served Yola and the villages to the South. Now in the third week the order was reversed.

Yola residents were delighted to see Mamdali's lorry full of life saving food. The cassava and millet bags were quickly off loaded and the food distributed to the villagers. There was no hurry to off load the maize, rice and sugar bags since piles of bags of these foodstuffs previously brought to the village were still lying in the backyard of the chairman's house. Mamdali, in the meantime, was waiting for the psychological moment to launch his calculated conversation with the Chairman.

It was 7 p.m., and the villagers who had come for their rations had dispersed. Chairman Lihimba with the characteristic hospitality of the Wampoto, invited Mamdali into his house for a cup of tea. This was the psychological moment Mamdali had been waiting for. Taking his small transistor radio with him, he entered Lihimba's house and sat down. Radio Kondowe was broadcasting the 7 O'clock news. Chairman Lihimba and his family were delighted to listen to the news broadcast; for it was the first time for them to listen to a radio since the family radio had been exchanged for food four months earlier.

'You like the radio, Mr. Chairman?' began Mamdali.

'Oh, it's a nice little thing. I had a slightly bigger one, but had to exchange it for food four months ago.'

'Sorry about that. But if you like, you may keep this one. I only use it when I'm on safari; and I've several of these at home.'

'Oh, thank you very much.'

'By the way, do you have enough food for your family.'

'I bought a bag of maize and a few measures of rice the first week, but the maize is almost finished now, and the rice got finished some days ago. You see, we have the so-called extended families and in situations like this, one has to mind one's relatives.'

'I tell you what, if you want rice or maize or sugar for yourself,

I can give you.'

'You mean you've got foodstuff of your own you're prepared to give me?'

'No, I mean I can give you money with which to buy the foodstuff.'

'Are you lending me the money or giving it to me free?'

'Well, I'll give you the money free, and you buy the food you need. Then I'll give you more money, the equivalent of the price of the food I have in the lorry, and you will allow me to take away those bags.'

'I see. So that's why you offered to give me your radio, and that's why you want to give me money. You're a very cunning fox. You know that this relief food is being sold to us by the government at reduced price. So you want to buy this food cheaply and resell it at your own price, eh?'

'What's wrong with that, my friend? You get something and I get something.'

'My name is Lihimba, which in our vernacular means lion. I cannot allow you to make a profit and grow fat on the poverty of my people. We are poor people, and we can't afford to buy the food the government has offered us, even at this give away price. But we are sending a delegation to Lusuma to ask the Governor to allow us to distribute this food to the people on credit terms. We're sure, given a year or two, we'll be able to pay the debt.'

'But what're you afraid of, my friend? What the government wants is to get back its money. I give you the full amount of money for these bags and you remit the money to Lusuma. The government will not want to know who actually bought the food.'

'Shut up! You think you can play with me? I've told you that my name is *lion*. I can devour you! The government is not interested in simply getting its money. It is interested in helping the citizens. If it were not so, why should government sell the food at such a low price?'

'Alright my friend, let's not quarrel. You and your people will die eating *makopa* and millet…'

'Don't make me angry! Remove your radio, and get out of my house! But make sure you leave all the bags you have in the lorry, here. By the way, have you been doing this kind of thing in the villages you've been to?'

'Oh, yes, of course. Your friends Mahinya, Litunu, and Mponda have plenty of food now because they followed my advice. Each week they've been remitting to Lusuma the full amounts of money for the bags I bought.'

'I see…. And each time you've been returning to Lusuma with the bags of food?'

'Of course! Look here Mr. Lihimba, this time I'll leave all the bags here, since you seem to be adamant. But I want you to think about it and let me know next week if you've changed your mind.'

'Alright, I'll think about it…'

Gulamali Mamdali left Yola village late that night. He was disappointed at the stubbornness of Chairman Lihimba, but the conversation had ended on a rather optimistic note. Hadn't the Chairman promised to think about it? Would he really persist in his stubbornness? The following week would show.

Early the following morning Chairman Lihimba wrote a long letter to the Provincial Governor. In it he described in detail the racket that was going on between Gulamali Mamdali and some of the village chairmen. He mentioned the proposition that Mamdali had made to him, and suggested that a trap be laid to catch Mamdali while returning to Lusuma the following week. He, Gaidon

Lihimba, would pretend to comply with Mamdali's suggestion by obtaining money from him and allowing him to take away the bags of food. To make the trap fool proof Lihimba suggested that all the bags that would be issued to Mamdali by the central stores at Lusuma should be carefully marked in order to provide proof afterwards that he had returned with the same bags he had been issued. Lihimba suggested further that a surprise inspection by the police be made of the homes of the suspected village chairmen to see how much food they had for themselves.

A young courier was dispatched with the letter to the Provincial Governor. It took him two days to reach Lusuma on foot. The letter was duly delivered and the governor having studied it carefully gave instructions to the police to lay a foolproof trap to catch the culprit.

When Mamdali collected his cargo from the provincial stores the following week, he had no idea that the bags had been carefully marked. It was also known that he would be returning to Lusuma during the night of the following day. A detachment of four policemen was ordered to waylay him on the way; and as there was no alternative route which Mamdali might take, the four policemen were hundred per cent sure of catching their man. At a point midway between Msamala village and Ngerenge church station, the policemen erected a roadblock, and waited for Mamdali.

As usual, Mamdali arrived at Yola village late in the afternoon, and the village residents as usual, queued for their weekly rations of dried cassava and millet. After they had dispersed, Lihimba invited his guest for a cup of tea, and without wasting time Lihimba introduced the subject of their conversation the previous week.

"My friend," began the Chairman, "I consulted my wife and children about the proposition you made the other day. We've decided to go along with it, after all, if others have done it why shouldn't I?"

"Now you speak like a wise man, my friend. What's important is simply to ensure that you remit to government all the money I give you for the bags. Don't keep a cent for yourself, for the bags have been counted and their price is known. You see, if the government had wanted to be sure that the food was bought only by your villagers, receipt books would have been issued in which you'd have to record the names of the recepients, and which you'd have to countersign. As it is, the government didn't bother about issuing receipt books. So you can take if from me that nobody's going to query you about this."

"We've thought about all this. Well then, let's get down to business. First, I must be sure how many bags of each foodstuff you have in the lorry."

"Sure, you may make a physical count of the bags in the lorry if you like. My turnboy will help you identify the different kinds of foodstuff. But if you trust me, you don't have to go to all that trouble, for here I have the papers showing the number of bags of maize, rice, sugar, cassava and millet that were issued to me at Lusuma."

"Fine, maybe it is not necessary for me to count the bags physically. I'll trust the figures shown in the issue notes."

With that settled, Mamdali produced a huge stack of ten thousand shilling notes and put it on the table. A quick multiplication and addition exercise gave the total cash value of the foodstuff. Lihimba counted the money and after satisfying himself that it was correct he took it away for safe keeping.

Shortly after 8 p.m. Mamdali left Yola. How he wished this operation would continue for another month or two! He would fill his godown at Lusuma with cheaply obtained food, and when the time came to resell it, money would begin rolling in! He would not sell all the food in Kondowe, there were countries, he knew, where a bag of rice could cost six times as much as it did in Kondowe. In Ushisha, for instance, rice was such a delicacy that he would have no trouble making six times as much money as he would in Kondowe! He would write his brother, Gulamali Pondamali, who lived in Lundo, the capital of Ushisha, to arrange things.

The night journey from Yola was uneventful. Mamdali used all his driving skill in negotiating the dangerous corners in the road as he climbed the Livingstone mountains. He didn't want the lorry overturning, for that would mean exposing the valuable cargo to passers by and giving rise to suspicion as to why the bags of food were being moved in the wrong direction!

He reached Msamala village shortly after midnight, and stopped there for a while to put water in his radiator. A little distance from the road he could see the parking lights of what looked like a lorry and two figures standing nearby. One of the figures was holding a hurricane lamp, while the other was giving directions to a third person inside the lorry. Presently Mamdali heard the thud of a falling bag. As an experienced transporter he knew at once that somebody was off loading bags of something. But who was he, and what cargo was it? Mamdali was curious to find out. He sent his turnboy to find out whose lorry the other one was, and what cargo was being off loaded. The turnboy was able to learn that the lorry was Mchakamchaka's, for the person holding the hurricane lamp was none other than his driver Mathias Nyoka. He also learned that two bags of rice had been offloaded.

This information gave Mamdali secret joy, for he knew that he was not alone in this racket. He started the engine. In another three hours, if all went well, he would be reaching Lusuma. As he approached the narrow bridge over river Mkuruchi which passes between Msamala village and Ngerenge church station, to his utter dismay, he noticed a strong roadblock. Damn this roadblock! What fool could've done this? Could this be the work of some rural lunatic? He brought his lorry to a stop and waited for his turnboy to get down and remove the roadblock. The turnboy had just touched the pole across the road when policemen emerged from the side of the road.

"Stop!" Shouted Sgt. Wilhem, their leader, as he pushed the turnboy aside. Then looking up at the driver of the lorry he commanded, "Dim your lights, surrender your switch, and get down!"

Mamdali did as he was commanded to do. He was then ordered to unlock the cargo compartment of the lorry; and with the help of a torch, the police were able to see the contents of the lorry. With the exception of the cassava and millet bags that had been offloaded at Yola, the lorry was intact with valuable bags of maize, rice and sugar!

"So this is how you make money, eh?" Asked Sgt. Wilhem without looking at Mamdali.

"Sir, I will explain." replied Mamdali.

"Explain what? I'm not a magistrate. You'll do all the explaining to the magistrate, not to me."

"But why the magistrate? You talk as if you have caught a suspect! When you hear what I've to tell you, you'll have to apologise to me for what you have just said, sir."

"Look here my dear man, my orders are not to discuss anything with you. Here, take your switch and drive your lorry. A few yards from here you'll see our two landrovers. One landrover will go in front, you will follow behind it, and the other landrover will follow behind you. Is that clear?"

"Alright sir, but there is really no meaning in all this. You see, I was asked by the villagers to return the food to the government stores at Lusuma because they have nowhere to store it in the village. The villagers have no money with which to buy the food even at the reduced price. As a matter of fact, even now they have piles of bags lying in the villages because they can't afford to buy the food."

"Very well. You're a very innocent man, then. You say this to the magistrate, and he will acquit you, and you can then sue the government for defamation of character, and you'll be awarded damages. Now come on, start off!"

✲✲✲

When the case, the Republic Vs Gulamali Mamdali was heard, Chairman Lihimba was the star witness for the prosecution. He produced in court all the money he had received from Gulamali Mamdali and gave a detailed account of the conversation he had had with him . In court too were Chairmen Mahinya, Litunu and Mponda. The case proved to be a brief one, for the accused village chairmen readily admitted having fallen into temptation because of the particularly difficult circumstances in which they found themselves. The magistrate was sympathetic with the village chairmen and gave them a strong warning never to do that kind of thing in future. But he took a serious view of Mamdali's behavior. An order was given to confiscate all the food he had stocked in his godown, and the money remitted to the government through the village chairmen was not returned to him. In addition, he was sentenced to two years in jail.

Five

Three years after what had been nicknamed the locust famine, life in the villages of Unyanja returned to normal. Gaidon Lihimba was still chairman of Yola village, but because of their involvement in the food racket during the famine days, Mahinya had been replaced by Chengula as chairman of Ngumbo village, and Litunu had also been voted out of office in his own village. In the Republic of Kondowe the office of village chairman carried no monetary reward to speak of. But it was a highly coveted one among the rural population because of the prestige it gave to the incumbents, and the privileges it offered them. For instance, on national days, and the Republic of Kondowe had many such days, the village chairmen were often invited to the Provincial headquarters at government expense, and there they were given V.I.P. treatment. When important visitors happened to pass through the villages it was the honour and privilege of the village chairmen to be the hosts. For this reason, they were given a small allowance annually. Also during all formal occasions like marriages, burials and other rituals, the village chairmen were always expected to play leadership roles.

  Mahinya and Litunu did not enjoy their reduced status as

ordinary villagers; for, having been chairmen of their respective villages for more than five years, they had reached the stage when they started imagining that without them their villages would be less prosperous than they were! How could they adjust themselves to life as ordinary villagers? They knew that it was Lihimba who had been the cause of their present trouble. To them, Lihimba was a stinking hypocrite who had acted out of jealousy. He had informed the Provincial Governor about Mamdali's activities simply because he had been told that Mahinya, Litunu and Mponda had plenty of food. But what had he gained by so doing, after all? Nothing. He may have succeeded in putting Mamdali in prison; and of course, he may have succeeded in removing Mahinya and Litunu from their village chairmanship, but there was nothing he had gained personally. Mahinya and Litunu talked about this whenever they met. They were embittered by Lihimba's role in the Mamdali case and they vowed to avenge Lihimba's disrespect for them by spoiling his name. But they had to be careful how they did it, for Lihimba was a highly respected person not only in Yola but also in the other villages like Ngumbo where his daughter Huka was married.

A number of intrigues were made against Lihimba. One morning when Lihimba entered his goat shed he found among his flock a goat that did not belong to him. How had it got mixed with his flock? Lihimba sent his children to every home, which owned goats to enquire if anybody was missing a goat. The owner, a widower who lived about a mile from Lihimba, was found in the end and the goat was restored to him. But the widower was unable to explain how his goat could have strayed so far away from home, unless somebody had stolen it and left it in Lihimba's shed. On another occasion, a Yola fisherman named Chawanda went down to the beach late in the evening intending to go fishing. He entered his beach hut to collect his net, but the net was nowhere to be seen. Now to a poor fisherman in one of these villages, the loss of a fishnet meant the loss of the only means of livelihood! He ran to Chairman Lihimba's home to report his loss, and both he and Lihimba started making enquiries about the missing net. They returned to the beach and made a thorough search of all the beach huts used for storing fishing gear. Chawanda's net was nowhere to be found. The search was resumed the next morning, and to everybody's amazement, Chawanda's little net was found tucked away in Lihimba's beach hut, although when the same hut had been searched the previous evening, nothing had been found! It was most embarrassing for Lihimba that the net should be found in his beach hut. But everybody in Yola, including Chawanda, knew that their chairman could not have done this. It must have been the work of some wicked person, probably from outside the village.

Lihimba himself began to suspect that somebody was scheming against him; first a stray goat mysteriously got mixed with his flock; and now Chawanda's net finds its way into his beach hut. Somebody must be playing tricks. But who was he, and what were his motives? Was he a fellow resident of Yola Village or a person from another village? Lihimba's suspicions were to be confirmed the following week.

Charles Nkomola of Ngumbo village was a close friend of Lihimba. They had grown up together, and in their younger days they had traveled to Lilungu together and worked there as junior clerks. Now though living in their respective villages, there wasn't a week that went by without their meeting to chat. It so happened that Charles had brewed *pombe* at his home and had invited a number of people to help him drag his newly made canoe from the foothills to the beach.

When a Mpoto tribesman has a big piece of work to do but feels he cannot cope with it alone, he brews a pot or two of good bubbling beer, popularly known as *pombe*. Then he formally notifies a trusted friend that he has a piece of work he needs to be done, for which he has prepared *pombe*. The kinds of jobs that one may wish to be done are the ordinary chores like cultivating a *shamba*, putting new thatch on the roof, building a house, mending a net, and so on. It is then left to the trusted friend so notified to invite a group of people to help do the job. The formal notification to the trusted friend is known as *ngokelu*. The Wampoto talk of *ngokelu* having been given to so and so meaning that somebody has been formally notified to send help to a friend. It is regarded as a matter of great honour to be given formal notification to send help to a friend. The person who gets the formal notification, in effect, becomes the guest of honour on the day the job is done; and after the job is done, the pots of bubbling beer are formally presented to him, and he shares the drink with the people who accompanied him.

Charles Nkomola had worked for several weeks making a new dug out canoe. The job of making a canoe is a tedious one. He had combed the bush to locate a tree suitable for canoe making; then he had felled the tree and chopped off the branches. Then followed the hard work of making the log hollow. Now a person may do all these things on his own or with the help of a friend, but when it comes to dragging the half-finished canoe to the beach, it is necessary to have many people together to do the pulling and pushing. Normally the finishing touches of smoothening the surface and straightening the shape of the canoe are done at the beach. So, Nkomola brewed three large pots of *pombe* and formally notified Mr. Malela, a trusted friend from the same village, about the date and the job to be done. He also sent a word to his friend Lihimba to come along and join in the drinking. As a matter of fact, Nkomola made sure he had a small pot of *pombe* specifically reserved for his friend Gaidon Lihimba.

After a hard day's work of pulling and pushing the heavy half finished log of a canoe to the beach from the foothills three miles away, Malela and his invitees settled down under a mango tree just outside Nkomola's house to enjoy their much deserved drink. Gaidon Lihimba who had arrived early that morning and had also given a hand in dragging the canoe was shown into a room in Nkomola's house, and there he spent the afternoon eating and drinking and cracking jokes with Nkomola's aging father. The drinking continued until late in the evening. Those drinking under the mango tree now started singing and talking animatedly. The drink was having the desired effect. At about 7 p.m. Gaidon Lihimba decided he'd had enough and it was time he left. So, saying goodnight to his good friend Nkomola and his wife, he started off for Yola. It was getting dark, but he had no difficulty walking along the road, which he knew so well.

He had walked only a few hundred yards from Nkomola's house when he heard somebody calling him from behind, '*Mzee*, please wait for me, I don't want to walk this distance to my house alone. I'm lucky to have your company.'

The voice was that of a woman who appeared to have taken a drop too many. Gaidon stopped to see who was coming. Presently the woman joined him. She was Lucresia, the wife of one Jonathan Matupila. Mrs Matupila was not a woman who could be described as virtuous. She was known all over Ngumbo and the neighbouring villages to be of loose character. Being childless, she often felt that she was not bound to stay at home like other married women. Her husband, she felt, could as well take care of himself. Whenever there was a *pombe* party in Ngumbo or any of the neighbouring villages you could almost be sure of finding Mrs Matupila there.

"Oh, how are you, Mrs. Matupila?" Asked Mr. Lihimba.

"Very well, and how's everybody in Yola?"

"Well, so, so… Were you also at Nkomola's?"

"Yes, of course. Where else should I have been, with all that nice *pombe* there?"

"Why are you leaving so soon, then? Have you had enough?"

"Enough what? *Pombe?* Oh, no, *pombe* is never enough for me. It's only that I was afraid walking home alone in the dark. So when I saw you leaving I decided I'd take advantage of your company."

"Fair enough. But tell me, Lucresia, why is it that we so often hear about you? You quarrel with men at *pombe* parties, and you do shameful deeds every now and then. Don't you realize you make your husband unhappy? I know Jonathan very well. He is a nice man, but you keep embarrassing him."

"What has my husband to do with you!" Screamed the drunken woman. "And why must you elderly people keep poking your noses in other people's affairs? You don't seem to know me, I'm going to teach you a lesson never again to try to be godfather to everybody!"

With that, she began to scream at the top of her voice; "*Yoyooo, mleteee*! *Yoyooo, mleteee*, please help, I'm being killed! Lihimba's killing me!"

The screams were heard by the people who were still drinking outside Nkomola's house, and they rushed towards the screaming woman, some of them carrying sticks and stones. When Lucresia heard the crowd rushing towards her she threw her *khanga* on the grass beside the road and partly tore her dress. Then she flung herself onto Lihimba and clung on him as if there was a scuffle between them. Gaidon Lihimba was completely at a loss to understand why the woman was behaving that way. His immediate thought was that the woman was having a fit of hysteria. As he tried to disengage himself from her, she clang to him more firmly, and when the mob reached them Lucresia cried out that Lihimba was trying to rape her! There could be no greater embarrassment for Lihimba than this, especially as his own son-in-law Jerome Kawacha, was among the people in the crowd. His friend Nkomola who was also in the crowd quickly stepped between the struggling pair and separated them. Then he turned to face the mob and said, "I know we all have had enough *pombe,* but that's no reason why we should behave irresponsibly now. Throw those sticks and stones away and let's hear what Lucresia has to say."

"We don't have to waste time listening to Lucresia," said a rugged looking young man. "The matter is clear, Lihimba was trying to rape her. Don't you see her torn dress and her *khanga* on the grass?"

"There's no doubt that's what he was trying to do," added another. "According to our custom, this man must be tied with rope and brought before the court. What're we waiting for?"

Saying this he produced a neatly folded piece of rope from his pocket and dashed towards Lihimba with the intention of tying his arms. Nkomola would have none of this. He released a tremendous right hook, which connected with the chin of the half drunken young ruffian and sent him slumping to the ground. Meanwhile Jerome Kawacha tackled the other rugged looking young man who had mentioned rape. To Jerome this was the greatest insult that anybody could have hurled at his father-in-law. He punched the young man's face and left an ugly lump just above the left eye. The young man defended himself by throwing punches everywhere without directing them to a particular target. But in so carelessly throwing his punches, the poor chap inadvertently hit Nelson Buka Livova, alias Nyundo, which means hammer. Now Nyundo was a household name in the whole of Unyanja, for he was feared by everybody on account of his strength. It was well known that one punch on the head by Livova was enough to fracture anybody's skull. Indeed, when people greeted him they normally refrained from shaking hands with him for fear that he might break their fingers. When the half drunken young man's fist landed on Livova's belly, Livova decided not to retaliate by punching back, instead he simply got hold of the chap's arm, twisted it, and with a slight push sent him falling to the ground face downwards. Although in Nyundo's opinion the push was only slight, its effect on the young rascal was to badly injure his face, bloody his nose, and break two teeth!

Malela, the guest of honour at Nkomola's *pombe* party, felt it his duty to restore peace. He shouted, entreating everybody to stop fighting. When everybody had quietened down he continued, "Is there anybody who doesn't know Gaidon Lihimba? And is there anybody who doesn't know Lucresia? Lucresia is a harlot and a drunkard. There isn't a *pombe* party she misses. There isn't a month that passes by without our hearing about her shameful deeds. But have you heard anything shameful about Lihimba? I have known Lihimba since his youth. You could never find a more respectful person in the whole of Unyanja. What this woman has done is a frame up. I can't believe anything she has said."

"Aa, but we've seen him with our own eyes struggling with her at this lonely spot and at this late hour! How can you suggest that he is innocent?" persisted the rascal that Nkomola had floored.

"Well, let's hear from Mr. Lihimba," suggested Malela.

Mr. Lihimba then calmly recounted all that had happened from the time he had left Nkomola's home. When he recalled the way Lucresia began removing her clothes and tearing her dress, and screaming, Malela interrupted, "You see, I told you, this is a frame up Lucresia is capable of doing such things. However, let's also hear from you, Lucresia."

Lucresia then gave her version of the story stressing that after she had joined Lihimba he made advances at her and when she refused he started attacking her.

"Since the woman says she was attacked, the matter must go to court," observed a bystander. "The court will decide who is telling the truth."

"Fine," agreed Nkomola. "Let's escort them to Chengula's house to have their statements taken."

When this was settled the whole party moved to the house of Mr. Chengula who was the new Village Chairman as well as the magistrate of the local Primary Court. Statements were taken and the case was heard on the third day.

The little courtroom of Ngumbo village was filled to capacity as the villagers strained their ears to catch every word that was being said in connection with Lihimba's case. Villagers from Yola who had arrived early that morning were determined to see that justice was done to their chairman.

Chairman Chengula read the statements made by Mrs Matupila and Mr. Lihimba, and then asked Mrs. Matupila to call her witnesses. She called the fellow who, on the fateful night, had produced the rope from his pocket, but had ended up slumping to the ground as a result of Nkomola's right hook. He went through the story again putting special emphasis on the fact that Lihimba was actually seen struggling with the woman, and that her khanga was found on the grass by the side of the road, and her dress was half torn. When he was cross-examined by Chairman Chengula he admitted that he had not picked up the rope from Nkomola's place, but had had it in his pocket from the time he left his own home. He admitted further that it was not his habit to carry ropes in his trouser pocket. He added, however, that on that particular day he had decided to carry the rope in case it was going to be needed for dragging the canoe.

At this juncture Mr. Malela stood up to speak. He wondered why if that fellow had carried that rope for the purpose of dragging the canoe he did not produce it when one was badly needed? As a matter of fact, at one point during the arduous task of dragging the canoe, Mr. Malela himself had asked if anybody had remembered to carry a rope, and seeing that nobody had, he had improvised by making one from a tree bark in the bush.

"Why didn't you say you were carrying a rope?" asked Malela.

"Well, when I was about to produce it, you had already made another rope from the *myombo* tree. So I decided to keep mine in the pocket."

"You must have carried that rope for a special purpose. You knew what was going to happen in the evening. Why don't you be bold enough to tell the court if you were hired?"

Mr. Chengula motioned to Mr. Malela whose temper was already rising, to sit down and hold his peace. The Chairman was about to call upon Mr. Nkomola to give his version of the story when Jonathan Matupila raised his hand to speak. He was given the floor. There was complete hush in the packed courtroom when Matupila stood up to speak, for everybody knew him to be the husband of the woman who had brought Lihimba to court.

"Ladies and gentlemen," began Jonathan Matupila, "one of the few things my late father taught me was to speak the truth no matter what the consequences. You all know my wife. You know the kind of life she and I lead. No month ever passes by without her being involved in some shameful deeds. I am a miserable creature on account of my wife…"

"Don't give us a general description of your life," interrupted Mr. Chengula. Tell us what you know about this case."

"Yes, sir, I'm coming to that. We all know Mr. Lihimba. When I heard about this thing that evening, I suspected at once that it was a frame up. You see, three days before this thing happened my wife brought home two hundred shillings. When I pressed her to tell me where she'd got the money from, she said she had been hired by somebody to do a job for him. I pressed her further to tell me what the job was, but she flatly refused to tell me. She simply said I should wait and see."

"But did she tell you who it was that had hired her to do the job?" asked the Chairman.

"Yes, she did. It was Mr. Mahinya."

At the mention of Mahinya there were murmurs all over the courtroom as people turned their head to look at him. Jonathan Matupila went on, 'I've told you that I was taught to tell the truth no matter what the consequences. I know, by revealing this, I've created enemies. I thought the truth had to be told. Mr. Mahinya gave my wife two hundred shillings and asked her to do a job for him. I don't know what the job was, but since he is here in court, perhaps he will care to tell the court what he hired my wife to do. My own suspicion is that he hired her to do what she did that evening!'

As people shouted, 'shame, shame', three men from Yola village left their seats and menacingly advanced towards Mahinya, but Chairman Chengula had seen them in time and he called them to order, threatening to sue them for contempt of court. When peace had been restored, Mr. Chengula called upon Mahinya to defend his honour. Mr. Mahinya stood up trembling with shame and uttered only one sentence, 'I've been taught one lesson today, never to trust a harlot.'

Lihimba looked at him and asked, 'The goat you put in my shed, and the net you left in my hut were not enough, and you had to sink so low?'

Mahinya had nothing to say. Then Chairman Chengula asked, "Did you also hire these two thugs to have a rope ready to tie Lihimba?" Again Mahinya had no answer to give.

* * *

As time went on animosity between Gaidon Lihimba and Mahinya grew more and more. Lihimba felt isolated, for although he enjoyed the popularity and respect of his own people in Yola, the same could not be said about the neighbouring villages where Mahinya and Litunu were doing everything in their power to discredit him. But Lihimba was also an ambitious man who did not define progress in esoteric philosophical terms, but in pragmatic terms to mean the possession of a modern house, clean water, food, clothing, means of transport, wealth, and so on. Now, partly because of the isolation he felt by being shunned by his fellow village chairmen who were influenced by Mahinya and Litunu, and partly because he saw no prospects for progress in Yola, Lihimba decided he would migrate to a distant place and start a new village. This was an idea he had nursed in his mind for some years, and now he felt the time was ripe for him to announce his intentions to the villagers in the hope of convincing a large number of them to follow him.

It was Sunday, and most of the Yola residents who were christians of the Anglican Church had gathered at their village school for prayers. Chairman Lihimba took advantage of the gathering by announcing that he had an important message to communicate to the villagers and asked them to proceed to the assembly *boma* as soon as the prayers were over.

When they were all assembled in the *boma*, Lihimba introduced the subject right away. "Comrades" he said, "I've been your chairman for the last eight years, and during all these years I've enjoyed your co-operation. We've lived like one united family. We've seen days of plenty and days of hardship. We've planned our lives together. You've always listened to me and I've listened to you. Today I'm not so sure that you'll all listen to what I'm going to say. As a matter of fact, I've wanted to tell you what I'm now going to say since the day I became the village chairman eight years ago, but I knew that the chances of being listened to then were very small, smaller than they may be today. Circumstances have changed and I feel morally bound to make my suggestion without fear. I'm suggesting to you all that time has come now when we should abandon this village and seek settlement elsewhere."

There were mixed murmurs in the crowd. The majority of the villagers simply could not believe that they had heard the last words of their chairman right. A number of elderly men shouted simultaneously, "Do what?"

"Leave the village and settle elsewhere," answered the Chairman.

"Where?"

"Well, that's what we can discuss at this meeting."

"Are you mad to suggest such a thing?" asked a voice.

"Don't call him mad, you fool," said Gaidon's young brother, Niklas Lihimba.

"Listen," shouted the Chairman, "I'm not mad, and as for you Niklas, you don't have to lose your temper and call him a fool. Be calm and I'll explain everything."

Josephat, who was the head teacher of the village primary school and who had at one time coveted the position of chairman, which Gaidon was holding, saw his chance of humiliating the Chairman.

He rose to speak, "Comrades, I hope you've all heard the Chairman's introductory remarks. He has said that he had wished to tell us to leave this village eight years ago, but for some reason, he couldn't do so". He added "I'd have understood the Chairman's feeling of consideration for our welfare if he had made this suggestion three years ago when we had the locust famine. But for him to make such a suggestion at a time when our village has already made remarkable recovery is, in my opinion, highly irresponsible. Such a move is bound to disrupt our community and plunge us into misery again."

"Josephat, I was expecting, you being an educated man, to listen to all I have to say before you begin antagonising the people to the idea I have put forward."

"Yes, it's because of my education that I feel I must object to your silly ideas."

"You have no right to call his ideas silly, you fool," objected Niklas Lihimba. "If you were all that wise and clever why were you not elected chairman of this village?"

"Please don't begin to quarrel. Let's listen to the chairman," said Mama Susana, an elderly and respected widow.

"Alright, go on, we're listening," shouted a group of young

men. "Tell us why we should leave our village, and tell us where we should go."

"I'm going to put the facts before you, and it'll be up to each one of you to consider them and decide whether I'm speaking the truth or not. It is my considered opinion that our village does not have enough land to support us all. Here are the facts: the distance between the mouth of river Luholochi which marks the southern boundary of our village and the Nkile promontory which marks the northern extremity of our village, is six miles. The widest part from the lake shore to the rocky foothills is approximately three miles. That's to say that Yola village, our beloved village, is roughly eighteen square miles. But if you take away the sandy beach, the useless reed choked marshes; the rocky ground to the east; and if you disregard the built up area, then we are really left with roughly seven square miles of arable land. But as you know from experience, most of this arable land is sandy, and cassava and groundnuts are about the only crops that do well in it. The other crops: maize, millet, rice, beans and vegetables grow only in the valleys of our two rivers, the Luholochi and the Munyamachi. You know yourselves, I need not tell you this, how we have fragmented our *shambas* in these river valleys! The largest plot owned by any individual is one acre. The majority of what we call *shambas* are hardly half-acre plots! But there are two hundred and ten families in our village, with a total number of one thousand and fifty mouths to feed!"

"Don't call us mouths," shouted Mwalimu Josaphat, "call us people!"

"Don't interrupt him," countered Mama Susana. "We are people, yes, but we have mouths to be fed! Go on, Mr. Chairman."

"As I was saying, there are one thousand and fifty of us in this village, all waiting to be fed. But of these, only four hundred and fifty can be relied upon to produce food. The rest are children, the aged and the infirm. Given the little land we have, our able bodied people, especially the men, work on their *shambas* for only three months of the year, and then there is nothing left for them to do. The rest of the chores, like weeding and harvesting are usually left to the womenfolk. What do our men do for the rest of the year? Well, you know the answer. They either go fishing, or they drink *pombe,* or they are at a *ngoma*. I'm not saying that our men are naturally lazy. Not at all. It's simply that our land being so little, our *shambas* have, of necessity, to be tiny plots which do not offer our men enough challenge."

"Listen to him, he is telling you the truth!" Shouted Mama Suzana.

"Thank you Mama Susana… But the point that I really want to drive home to you, the point that should make any sensible person among you stop and think, is that our village land area is becoming smaller and smaller every year! We are at the mercy of the lake. One extraordinarily large wave is enough to overwhelm much of our village. Indeed, twenty years ago, Archdeacon Lamborne predicted that one wave a few meters high was enough to inundate half of all the land bordering this lake! Nor was this an idle dream. It has in fact been happening, albeit gradually. Many of us still remember that twenty years ago our primary school was farther than the rock you see out there in the lake! That rock is now about half a mile from the shore. This means that within twenty years the lake has been eating away much of our land. Even a fool knows this. What's going to prevent it from devouring the whole of our village? More than this, the present river valleys are not what they used to be. Formerly the two rivers were narrow, deep streams. Their banks have been collapsing year after year and the riverbeds have continued to broaden. While the lake is eating away our cultivable land, the rivers are also robbing us of our most valuable soil. We continue fragmenting what is left! How much land will be left ten years from now is anybody's guess. Comrades, let's act now in order to ensure a bright future for our children. The step we take now may be difficult, but I'm sure it will prove us right in the long run."

At this juncture there were spontaneous ululating sounds followed by prolonged hand clapping by some of the men.

"Listen to him," shouted Mama Susana. "He is quite right when he says that water is eating away our land. My groundnuts *shamba* used to be beyond that rock in the lake, and my rice field used to be somewhere in the middle of the present mouth of the Munyamachi river. I'm old, and I may soon be following my husband. So I don't really mind what happens to me now. But what's going to happen to our children and grandchildren? His words are words of wisdom. Act now while there's still time."

Mr. Sefu, a tall man in his sixties, and one who was greatly respected by his village mates since he happened to own the largest log canoe as well as the largest fishnet in the village, stood up to speak.

"Comrades," he said, "I've listened to the discussion until now, but I feel a little confused. I cannot make up my mind whether to follow the Chairman's advice or not. On the one hand, all he has said about this village is absolutely true, no one who knows this village can object to any of the things he has said. We all know quite well that our land is being eaten away by water. I grew up and tended my father's goats somewhere beyond the rock you see in the lake, there! I also remember quite well the village *shambas* we used to cultivate along the river valleys. But, on the other hand, comrades,

I've buried my parents and my children here. How do you expect me to abandon the graves of my people? Besides, we are fishermen, if we could concentrate on fishing we could obtain the other foodstuffs from other people, either by buying them with the money we obtain through fishing, or by exchanging our fish for the other foodstuffs. What I'm saying, in other words, is that we do not all have to be cultivators of land. We can make our living by fishing."

"Surely you cannot be serious Mr. Sefu," shouted Chawanda. You know very well that during the locust famine we thought we could exist by fishing, but we couldn't. It's all right for you to pin your hope on fishing since you have a large net and a big canoe. But what about the rest of us with only tiny old nets?"

Mr. Emilias who had been itching to speak now stood up. This man had lived in South Africa for ten years working in the mines, but had returned to Yola village six years ago. His greatest ambition while working in South Africa had been to buy his village modern drums such as are used by brass bands. He had managed to acquire one large drum and four small ones; these he brought home and gave them as a present to the village *ngoma* group. Of all the different kinds of *ngoma* played by the Wampoto, *mganda* or *lipenenga* is the most popular. What you need for this dance is a large round drum similar to those used by brass bands, plus one or two small ones. The Wampoto, of course, make their own drums using discarded petrol drums and cattle skin. But if you can use modern drums, so much the better; for these not only give better sound, but they also add prestige to the *ngoma* group. As a matter of fact, Mr. Emilias had also brought with him white gloves to be worn by the drummers! These presents had been appreciated so much by the villagers that they had unanimously elected Mr. Emilias 'king' of the dance group, a highly coveted position during dancing sessions.

Six years is a sufficiently long time for change to register in a person's physical appearance. Mr. Emilias who, six years ago, had returned to Yola as a prosperous looking young man, now looked rustic and older than his age. Just now he was sporting a tattered black felt hat, a tattered striped shirt and a pair of trousers, part of what was once an expensive flannel suit. The trousers loosely held by suspenders from the shoulders, had two large incongruous patches sewn roughly in the region of the two knees; and to protect his feet from the hot sand of the village, he had on the remains of what had once been a high quality pair of shoes. At least three toes of each foot were showing, and the shoe laces which had long been lost, had been replaced by string made from a local plant. He stood up and cleared his throat.

"Comrades," he said, "if the suggestion made by the Chairman is followed, it will mean only one thing, the disintegration of our community as we've always known it. I presume that not everybody will want to go to the place the Chairman has in mind. Some will probably want to go to places of their own choice. Indeed, some may not want to leave this village. Whatever happens, I fear our famous *mganda* group will be no more…"

"Look here," interrupted Jeremia Kahongi who was known to be a strong supporter of the Chairman, 'before you start weeping for your dear *ngoma*, why don't you wait to hear where the Chairman wants us to migrate to?"

"Yes," shouted a number of young men, "that's what we're waiting for. Tell us where you want us to go to, and we'll follow you!"

"Thank you, very much," answered the Chairman. "I'm greatly encouraged to hear you young people say so. The idea of starting a new village will stand or fall in accordance with your determination. If you are determined to make a success of life in a new environment I do not see why we shouldn't succeed. It is not necessary that everybody abandons this village immediately. The older folks and a few young men could remain behind. But if from every family in the village, at least one able bodied young man could volunteer to migrate, then we could have no less than two hundred pioneers to start the new settlement. Later on those left behind could follow and join us."

"Mr. Chairman," shouted the now enthusiastic crowd, "we have already told you that we are ready to start off even now. Tell us where you want us to go to."

"Very well, I'll tell you. Mind you, I don't want us to leave this village only to settle in another place where we shall be just as poor as we are here. We must choose a place where we can create wealth, a place with plenty of good land on which to grow cash crops. I want us to choose a place where, within the next ten years, each one of us will be able to make enough money out of the sweat of his brow."

"Our greatest problem in this village is that apart from fish, we have no other means of making money. We have no important cash crop. Groundnuts would have been an important cash crop if we could produce enough of it. But as you know, due to the scarcity of land, each one of us is able to produce just enough for domestic use."

"Now, the place I have in mind is not very far from here. If you go about fifteen miles up the Luholochi river you reach a place where both the Luholochi and the Munyamachi have their sources, although the actual springs from which both rivers rise are a little farther to the east on the Uhenga mountains. Between the two streams is an area approximately thirty square miles. It is an area of rich alluvial soil, even topography and excellent climate. The whole area is very thinly populated; for, as you know, the Wahenga prefer to live on the mountains. Almost everything can grow there; but coffee does exceptionally well in that soil. Chairman Kakoyo's village is perched up the mountains and he has no control over the few people living in the plain below."

"So, I'm almost sure we won't have any problem being welcomed by the few people dispersed over that area. This is all I had to tell you; and now I'm waiting for your reaction. But while you are making up your minds, I want you to remember that we are doing all this not only for ourselves but also for our children. Also remember that because we are doing this willingly, it will be possible for us to migrate orderly and gradually. If, someday, we were to be forced by government to abandon this village, and I don't see why the government couldn't do that for our own good, then it wouldn't be possible to do things in an orderly manner. Instead, the experience would be traumatic."

"Comrades," said Chawanda, "I know the place the Chairman is talking about. I'm ready to start off at once. That place is called Kindimba Juu. Everything grows there. I want to harvest my first crop of coffee five years from to-day. Kindimba Juu is not too far from here. If I want to come back and do a little fishing who's going to forbid me? As for those who think that *mganda* is so important that we should continue wearing rags in this village so long as we can play *mganda,* I say to hell with *mganda,* and to hell with their drums! Mr. Chairman, I am with you."

"I'm also ready to go," said Yeremia Kahongi.

"So am I," said Mzee Susa.

"If Susa goes, I also go," said medicine-man Bakari Mchope.

"So are we," shouted a group of young enthusiasts.

"Comrades," interrupted Mwalimu Josaphat, "before you get carried away by emotion, I want to remind you of one thing: you are forgetting, your children. What's going to happen to our children's schooling? If the parents migrate the children will have to follow them, and that will mean disrupting their schooling. Are you sure you're going to find a school for the children in the new village? As the chairman has said, the area you want to go to is very thinly populated and there is no primary school there. And even if you were to build one yourselves are you sure you would have the teachers, and the permission to have a school? Mind you, if some people migrate and others remain here it will mean that both this village and the new one will not have enough children to run a primary school. You see, to be permitted to have a primary school you need a certain minimum number of children. Below that number the local government will simply not allow you to start a primary school!"

"And what's the minimum number required?" asked Yeremia Kahongi.

"I don't know. I can't tell you off hand."

"Then don't tell us things you aren't sure of! Besides, the children don't have to come with us immediately. They can remain here with their mothers while we build the new village: and when they join us later they will find a school building waiting for them. Let no man here discourage us by pretending to know more than we do! As for obtaining permission from the local government, well, who are the local government? Aren't they people like us? We can talk things over with them. After all, isn't the local government encouraging people to develop? Surely they will not deny us permission to have a primary school once we have shown our determination by putting up a durable school building?"

Kahongi's emotional reply was greeted by prolonged applause while some people booed Mwalimu Josaphat.

The Chairman then suggested that the best thing to do was for all those who were definitely willing to go, to register their names. A notebook was produced, and young Niklas Lihimba took down the names of those who volunteered to go. At that meeting alone, two hundred and fifty names were registered. In the days that followed more names were recorded until the list hit the four hundredth mark.

Several other meetings were convened after the first one, at which details of the migration were worked out.

Six

Bakari Mchope reached for his goat skin bag. He took from it a tiny black horn, one end of which had been carefully sealed with black gum. He removed the gum and poured on the palm of his left hand a whitish powder. Then he sprinkled the powder onto the fire causing a thick white smoke to rise in the air. As the smoke began to rise, and the smell of the burning powder began to permeate the room he said, "With malice towards none, and friendship towards all, we come to this land. We want to found a new village in which our children and grandchildren will prosper. May the elders of this land receive us kindly.

"May our labours bear fruit. May those who harbour in their hearts malicious thoughts about us be struck down by lightning. May our progeny take root in this land, and may my prayer ascend to *Chiwuta* the way this smoke is ascending."

Susa, Chawanda, Kahongi and Gaidon Lihimba answered, "so be it." The five villagers from Yola were clustering round a log fire in Chairman Kakoyo's house. The time was 5 a.m. and it was bitterly cold outside. For people used to the warm weather of the lake shore, the cold on the Uhenga mountains at this time of the year, the end of July, was almost unbearable. That is why they had kept the fire burning throughout the night.

After the great debate in Yola at which the decision to move to a new village was made, a number of subsequent meetings had been held. One of the decisions taken at these meetings had been to send a delegation to Chairman Kakoyo to formally seek his permission and that of the other elders of Uhenga for the Yola emigrants to settle in Kindimba Juu. Although Kindimba Juu was a few miles from Kakoyo's village, and although it was thinly populated, the few people living there had, in fact, once belonged to Kakoyo. It would thus have been most unwise for the Yola villagers to superimpose themselves on another tribe without the consent of the host tribe. To do so would almost certainly have precipitated a feud between them.

The five-men delegation headed by Gaidon Lihimba had arrived at Chairman Kakoyo's home the previous evening. As is customary for most Kondowe tribesmen, visitors on an important mission like this carry presents for their hosts. Gaidon's party had carried a parcel of smoked fish for Chairman Kakoyo, and Kakoyo's eldest wife had duly received the present and shared it with the younger wives. Chairman Kakoyo, in turn had slaughtered a sheep for his guests, and after the guests had had a hearty meal, they had been shown into a room in the Chairman's main house in which to spend the night.

It was in this room that Bakari Mchope was now performing the ritual; and because of the cold, Bakari and Susa took turns in keeping the fire burning throughout the night. Bakari had wakened the group at 5 a.m. and started the ritual, which was the reason why Bakari Mchope had been voted a member of the delegation, so that he would perform this ritual.

The house in which the visitors from Yola had spent the night was a huge structure built of burnt brick. Although the inside walls had no plaster, in Gaidon's view, this house was better than anything one could see in the whole of Unyanja. It had a roof of corrugated iron sheets and a cement floor. At least two of the front windows had glass panes, although the rest of the windows were wooden ones. The doors and most of the furniture were made of excellent *mninga* wood. Gaidon had noted all these details about the house, and as soon as Bakari had finished his brief ritual, he jokingly began to taunt his comrades.

"Susa, have you ever slept in a house like this before?" he asked.

"Only once when I was admitted into Saint Theresa hospital at Namatui ten years ago." They all laughed.

"And you, Chawanda?"

"Not at all. This is my first time. But you wait and see, I'll build one like this before I die."

"And do you know how long you've still got to live?"

"I'm not all that old. I expect to live for at least another twenty years."

"How much would a house like this cost?" asked Kahongi.

"Probably thirty thousand shillings." Answered Gaidon.

"Oh, as much as that? How can one save thirty thousand shillings?"

"It's not impossible. You see, people like our host, can easily make more than thirty thousand shillings a year. One year's sale of coffee can bring that amount, depending, of course, on the amount and quality of the coffee harvested. Did you notice the coffee *shamba* as we approached the house? Now, that *shamba* is probably three acres, and a good yield from a three-acre *shamba* can easily bring thirty thousand shillings."

"How do these people get cement and corrugated iron sheets and glass?" asked Bakari Mchope.

"What do you think?" countered Gaidon. "You think they ask *Chiwuta* to send them these materials from the clouds like rain? No. They buy them from Lusuma. These people here own lorries; so once they've sold their coffee they go to Lusuma, buy these materials, load them in their lorries, and bring them here. I do hope you understand now what I meant back home when I said that we should seek better opportunities elsewhere. Without cash crops, you can'`t make enough money to buy such things."

"Do you think we're going to make enough money to buy lorries and build houses like this?" asked Kahongi.

"Why not? We may not be able to buy lorries, but one lorry, yes. I don't see why, ten years from now, we shouldn't be able to afford a lorry for our village if we work hard enough. As for owning decent houses, I should like us to accomplish this in the next four to five years. Remember the timetable we've set for ourselves. We must stick to it strictly. But all these things will remain dreams unless we translate our intentions into action. We'll have to work extremely hard and exercise iron discipline if we want our dreams to come true."

"By the way," said Susa, "what's likely to happen when we meet the elders later this morning? We haven't discussed this. We must prepare our answers together, so we can all speak with one voice."

"You're quite right, Susa. I was going to go into that," answered Gaidon. "What's likely going to happen is that Chairman Kakoyo will call the village government which, I'm told, consists of all the heads of the major clans in this village. They will then want to hear from us what our plans are. I'll take care of that. I do not envisage any problem arising out of the meeting. The important thing is for us to assure them that we shall be good neighbours who will be ready to co-operate with them in every way."

"We shall leave you to do most of the talking. But if they want any of us to say something, we'll be ready for them," said Susa.

At nine o'clock Chairman Kakoyo asked the visitors to accompany him to the *baraza* which was a mile away from his home. The assembly hall, unlike the bamboo *boma* of Yola, was a dilapidated brick building built during the colonial days. In those days such public buildings popularly known as *mabaraza* were the nerve centres of local government activity; for they served as law courts, tax collecting centres, assembly halls, and as offices for all the local government departments.

After the five visitors had been shown to their seats inside the *baraza*, the village elders, ten of them including Chairman Kakoyo, took theirs, on a raised platform. The meeting turned out to be easier than the visitors had anticipated. Chairman Kakoyo quickly introduced the subject of the meeting by recalling the plight of some of the Wampoto during the locust famine. He mentioned something about the scarcity of land in Unyanja, and noted with satisfaction the determination of the visitors and their people back home to improve their lot through hard work. He informed his village-mates about the visitors' intention to seek permission to settle in Kindimba Juu, and hinted that as far as he was concerned, he saw no reason why these people should not be allowed to settle in Kindimba Juu where there was plenty of unoccupied land.

There was very little debate on the matter. One counsellor wanted to know how many people were thinking of moving to Kindimba Juu, and Gaidon Lihimba promptly answered that so far only two hundred people had indicated they would migrate. However, he was hopeful that as time went on more people would move into the new village. He did not, however, envisage all the residents of Yola village moving to Kindimba Juu, as there were those who could not countenance life away from the lake and from fishing.

Another counsellor wanted to know if the newcomers would be prepared to follow some of the practices of the Wahenga, especially with regard to the use of land. For instance, he pointed out, the Wahenga had developed a special method of cultivating which enabled them to completely prevent soil erosion and preserve the fertility of the soil. For instance, he went on, it was taboo among the Wahenga to burn grass. Bush fires, which were common in Unyanja, were unknown in Uhenga. He wanted to satisfy himself that the Wampoto would observe these practices which, to his mind, were crucial for the conservation of land, which next to man, was the most important natural resource. To all these, Gaidon gave the necessary assurances.

A third counsellor, a lady and a descedant of the former paramount chief of the Wahenga, was more interested in social matters. She wanted to know if the Wampoto would be prepared to marry Wahenga girls and if they would be prepared to allow their girls to be married by the Wahenga. This not only caused laughter in the *baraza*, but it prompted Suza to declare that if he was still eligible he would wish to marry two or more Wahenga girls.

On a more serious note, another counsellor warned the Wampoto against their antiquated beliefs in witchcraft. Such beliefs, he said, brought fear, which in turn hindered progress. If they were seriously thinking of developing, they had to throw away their charms and *tunguli*.

To this Bakari Mchope replied simply that they would see to it that anybody with such beliefs was not allowed to settle in

Kindimba Juu.

Chairman Kakoyo finally summed up the discussion by stressing that while the Wahenga warmly welcomed the Wampoto into Kindimba juu, it did not mean that the few Wahenga living in the area should be displaced. The Wampoto were to settle only on unoccupied land. As there was plenty of land in Kindimba Juu he saw no reason why the indigenous residents there should be harassed by the newcomers on account of land. He also pledged the co-operation of his people, and expressed the hope that the new comers would show a similar spirit. Once accepted, the men from Yola built temporary huts to live in as they started life in the new village.

* * *

The building of Kindimba Juu started in earnest the following month. Gaidon Lihimba and his people had drawn up a timetable of activities to which they strictly adhered. The first year was spent mainly in preparing food crop *shambas* and building temporary dwelling places. They were careful not to make mistakes at the beginning, which would be difficult to correct later. For instance, in apportioning land among themselves they made sure that each person had at least an acre on which to build his house; six acres on which to grow food crops, and six acres on which to grow cash crops. Each grown up person had at least thirteen acres of land at his disposal. In addition, some communal land was reserved for grazing; and the areas bordering the rivers were left as forest reserves.

One of the first tasks to be tackled was to erect a fence round the whole area where the food crop *shambas* were located. The few Wahenga of Kindimba Juu had warned the newcomers that wild pigs were a constant menace in the area, as they could devastate whole *shambas* of food crops. Lihimba and his people resolved to tackle this problem together. They cut poles and bamboo and proceeded to erect the fence. Now, a fence for the protection of food crops against wild pigs need not be a high one. A one or two metre high fence is enough to keep them at bay.

Gaidon had divided his people into groups, and each day each group was assigned a specific task to do. For instance, while one group was erecting the fence, another was cultivating somebody's food *shamba*; another was building somebody's house, and another was given other duties like tending the animals, preparing food for those working in the fields, and so on.

Once each week they assembled to review the progress of their activities and to chart out new directions. It was on these occasions that Gaidon exhorted his village mates to work hard. It was a life and death struggle, he kept repeating. They had to succeed. The future was going to be bright.

The villagers heeded their leader's exhortations. Not a single person could be seen loitering in the village. Each day, as soon as they had taken their breakfast, which almost invariably consisted of *kande* and *uji,* they set off like soldiers to their various duties. At mid-day, food was brought to the fields and work was interrupted for one hour to allow the villagers to take their meal. Work was resumed after lunch and it continued up to 6 p.m. This was the daily routine throughout the week except on Wednesdays and Sundays, which were left free for people to be on their own. It did not mean that they had a holiday on Wednesdays, but each individual was supposed to attend to his own *shamba*. Sunday was observed as a day of prayer and rest. The villagers had decided right from the beginning that they would not have the so-called communal village farm. They had heard of such farms having failed elsewhere, so they decided to adopt the alternative method of *bega kwa bega* farming, cultivating one another's *shamba* together by turns.

By the end of the rainy season in April, healthy crops of maize, finger millet, cassava, rice and potatoes could be seen all over Kindimba Juu. None of the crops had been destroyed by the wild pigs as these had been effectively barred by the fence. Lihimba urged his people to build barns in which to store the foodstuffs, and in addition he suggested that they build two or three communal barns to which each villager would be required to contribute a fraction of his maize and rice harvest. The experience of the locust famine being still fresh in their minds, the villagers readily understood the importance of ensuring that they had food reserves in the village.

June and July were again months of intense activity for the villagers as they gathered into the barns the results of their labours. The communal barns built on a rocky hillock in the centre of the village were stocked to the brim with maize and rice.

As soon as the harvest season was over in mid-August, Chairman Lihimba announced a new rota for the year. This year emphasis would be placed on the preparation of coffee *shambas*. The long-term objective was that each Kindimba Juu resident should one day own one thousand coffee trees. But they realised it would not be possible for them to accomplish this in one year. So they resolved that each one of them should prepare five hundred holes between August and December, and that by February of the following year each one should have planted five hundred coffee seedlings. The target of having one thousand coffee trees for each person would be reached the following year. They realised too that their plan could hit a snag unless they sought advice either from the local inhabitants or from the government. The growing of coffee called for special expertise, and the Wampoto fishermen from the lake shore had no idea about coffee growing. They didn't know what size of holes to dig, what spacing between plant and plant was required, and how seedlings were raised. They had no idea about pruning coffee trees. They would have to learn all these things, and more.

Lihimba realised these were genuine problems about which he had to seek assistance. He consulted Chairman Kakoyo who readily agreed to ask his village mate Julias Lipaki, a retired agricultural instructor, to visit Kindimba Juu and demonstrate to the villagers how to start coffee growing. During his working days in the colonial times, Mr. Lipaki had visited almost every village in Uhenga instructing people how to grow coffee. Indeed, it was acknowledged publicly by all the Wahenga that he was the man who had been instrumental in spreading coffee as a cash crop in Uhenga. Now retired, he was living in his home village taking care of his ten acre coffee *shamba*. Julias agreed to spend a few days in Kindimba Juu to help the villagers, who in turn agreed to pay him a small fee for his service.

After Lipaki's demonstration, the villagers worked hard to prepare the holes for transplanting the seedlings. But there was the problem of getting the seedlings. Coffee seedlings are expensive to buy, and the Wahenga, hospitable as they were, were not prepared to part with five hundred seedlings for each Kindimba Juu resident. Gaidon Lihimba was undaunted. He left the village and journeyed to Lusuma where he managed to get an appointment with the Provincial Governor. He presented to the governor his request for coffee seedlings. The determination and initiative of this man impressed the sympathetic governor, especially when he heard all that had transpired since the locust famine. An order was given to the Provincial Agricultural Officer to issue Kindimba Juu villagers with free coffee seedlings from the government nursery, and have the seedlings sent to Kakoyo's village from where the Kindimba

Juu villagers would collect them. This was done, and by the end of February of the following year, every adult resident of Kindimba Juu village had planted five hundred coffee seedlings.

Similar efforts were made the following year, so that three years after these people had settled in Kindimba Juu each adult male had a coffee *shamba* of at least one thousand trees as well as a three acre *shamba* of food crops.

The following three years were years of consolidation for the Kindimba Juu settlers. For, while eagerly awaiting their first harvest of coffee, the villagers concentrated their efforts in making their life secure and comfortable. They cleared the bush and made a narrow road from Kindimba Juu to Kakoyo's village, thus making it possible for small vans to reach the village. Each resident expanded his food crop *shamba* and diversified the crops. They improved their dwelling places by replacing the initial temporary huts with semi-permanent pole and mud houses. They formed committees to deal with specific aspects of their life: an economic and planning committee to chart out strategies for economic development; a defence and security committee, and an education and welfare committee. They were careful not to have too many committees to start with, lest they should waste too much time talking rather than working. The economic and planning committee, which was by far the most important committee, was headed by Mr. Lihimba himself. This committee made plans for the diversification of the cash crops by introducing crops like tobacco and sunflower. It made plans to introduce exotic timber trees, which would be planted in the coffee *shambas* to provide shade to the coffee trees.

It mobilised the women and encouraged them to continue with their art of pottery for which they were famous; and it encouraged the men to indulge in basket making using bamboo plants which were plentiful in Kindimba Juu. Virtually every activity that could somehow increase the household finances was encouraged. Later the economic and planning committee suggested the building of a market place. A modest pole and mud market was built and it proved extremely successful, especially since it was possible to draw people from the heavily populated mountain areas.

Gaidon Lihimba made sure that each week a group of young men from the village went down to the lake to fish. The fish was carefully smoked or sun dried and brought to the market at Kindimba Juu. Fish became the greatest attraction to the Wahenga from the mountains. In addition, the market offered a wide range of pots and baskets. This way, the Wampoto, who three years ago had arrived in Kindimba Juu as poor fishermen with hardly a cent in their possession, began to experience the pleasure of possessing some money. They were encouraged. The economic and planning committee would later come out with more ambitious plans like starting a village shop, a carpentry workshop, and so on. But for the time being, these plans had to wait.

The defence and security committee was really no more than a group of young men whose responsibility was to report on vermin which might threaten the safety of the crops. These people had to inspect the fence surrounding the food crop *shambas* and report on any incursions of wild pigs into the *shambas*. There was really no need to keep an eye on possible human enemies, for, in these remote rural areas theft and hooliganism were virtually unknown.

The education and welfare committee dealt with everything from making plans to erect a three classroom school building, and negotiating with the Lusuma authorities to have a teacher appointed to the village school, to ensuring that health measures were followed by everybody. This committee controlled the brewing of *pombe* in order to ensure that too much food was not wasted, and that the village did not encourage drunkenness. Members of this committee also went around the village to ensure that each household had a pit latrine and kept its surroundings clean. It forbade people from bathing and washing clothes in the rivers lest they should contaminate the water, which was also used for drinking.

Seven

Three years after they had planted the first coffee seedlings, the coffee trees began to blossom, and the villagers were filled with excitement. They watched the bees and butterflies hover over the blossoms and they watched the little white petals fall to the ground. After the blossoms had disappeared, tiny green berries appeared. The berries grew bigger and bigger and their colour began to change from green to light green to red, and to dark red. They were ready for picking.

As soon as the picking season started, Julias Lipaki was at hand to show them how to handle the coffee berries: how to pluck them from the trees; how to remove the skin using small hand machines; how to clean the coffee beans; and most important of all, how to dry the beans. It was important, insisted Julias Lipaki, that they knew how to handle the berries and the beans properly from the time the berries were picked from the trees to the time the dried beans were put in bags ready for sale. He pointed out for instance, that the price of the coffee would be determined by two things: the size and colour of the beans, and the colour would depend upon the way the beans were dried. If they were exposed to too much sun, they would lose their colour, and therefore their quality. So, for best results, they had to be dried in the shade.

The villagers followed Lipaki's instructions to the letter. From morning to afternoon they toiled in the coffee shambas picking coffee berries. In the evenings they used their hand machines to separate the skin of the berries from the hard beans; then they washed the slippery beans in streams of water until they were quite clean before spreading them on large mats to dry. As instructed by Julias Lipaki, they were careful to dry the beans in the shade to ensure that they had the right colour.

The office of the Kondowe Coffee Authority at Lusuma began to buy coffee from Uhenga in September. Gaidon Lihimba had arranged with the coffee authority to have them buy coffee from Kindimba Juu, and have it carried in small vans to Kakoyo's village from where it would be loaded in lorries and transported to Lusuma.

* * *

It was a bright morning in late September. The Kindimba Juu villagers were gathered at their market place where they had brought their bags of coffee. This was no ordinary market day for, to-day, representatives of the Coffee Authority were coming to buy coffee from the village. Today, for the first time in their lives, most of these peasants were going to handle large sums of money. It is true, they had often sold fresh and smoked fish in Yola village, and it is true that since building their new market in Kindimba Juu they had sold things like pots, baskets and mats, but proceeds from these activities were nothing compared with the dough they were expecting today!

While the women folk were jealously guarding the bags of

coffee inside the market building, the men were gathered outside jubilantly chatting about what they were going to do with the money they were about to get.

"How many bags have you got, Chawanda?" Asked Niklas Lihimba.

"Fifty."

"That'll probably be two thousand five hundred kilos."

"And how much am I likely to get, you think?"

"That'll depend upon the grade of the coffee. If it's all grade one, you could get twenty five thousand shillings, since a grade one kilo is ten shillings."

"What did you say, twenty five thousand?" Goodness, isn't that a real *donge?* If I get that, you'll all know me as Chawanda the son of Lipanga!"

"But if your coffee is of low grade," continued Niklas, "you could end up getting much less than that amount."

"Even if I get half of that amount I'll still be happy, and you will still recognise me as Chawanda *bin* Lipanga!'

"Hey, how about you Susa, how many have you got?" Asked Niklas Lihimba.

"Sixty bags."

"You could realize thirty thousand shillings if all your coffee is first grade. I'm expecting that much. My cofee is first grade. The beans are big, and the colour is just as they said it should be, grey. You see, I was very careful not to expose the beans to too much sun."

"And what're you going to do with all that money *Mzee* Susa?"

"Don't worry about that. I know what I'm going to do with it, alright."

"I think I know what you mean."

"What?"

"It's rumoured that you want to marry a Mhenga woman. Is that true?"

"Oh, not only one, but two! With that kind of dough I think I can afford to have two wives."

"Susa!" Interrupted Gaidon Lihimba who had been listening to the idle chatter, "you seem to have already forgotten all the nice plans we've made for our future. In stead, you start thinking about wives even before you've got the money!"

"What plans?"

"The plans to build modern houses, to buy a lorry, to start a shop and a carpentry workshop, and to have piped water. Have you forgotten these plans so soon?"

"Well, how about my plan to have two Wahenga wives? Is this not a plan? Remember I told the Wahenga elders the first time we visited Kakoyo that I intended to marry two Wahenga wives? This is important. It'll be good public relations if I become the son-in-law of two Wahenga elders!"

As they were thus chatting, and Susa was ineffectually trying to justify his plan to marry two wives of the Wahenga tribe, Kahongi who had been scanning the mountain road suddenly shouted, "They're coming!" They saw a trail of dust above the mountain road. It took twenty minutes for the two vans to reach the market place. Four clerks alighted from the two vans. After they had been welcomed by the villagers the clerks offloaded a heavy iron box from one of the vans, and carried it into the market building. Then with the help of the villagers they offloaded a heavy weighing machine, a large sieve, two large wooden containers, and a bundle of gummy bags.

Chairman Lihimba had, with his usual thoroughness, prepared

a complete list of the names of all the heads of households, which he handed over to the head clerk. Then the names were called out one by one. The first task was to grade the coffee. The large sieve was placed over one of the wooden containers and each peasant in turn was required to spread his coffee beans on the sieve. The beans that passed through the sieve were graded number two, while those that did not pass through were graded number one. But this applied only to cofee which was judged to have the right colour. If the coffee was judged to be of inferior colour, the whole consignment was graded number two, no matter what the size of the beans.

Fortunately for the peasants, the criterion of colour was not very critical since most of the coffee was found to have the right colour as it had been dried in the shade. It did however affect one peasant who, having finished picking his coffee late, had hurried to beat the deadline by drying his coffee in the sun. By so doing he had caused at least five bags of his coffee to be graded number two on account of the poor colour of the beans. As for the rest of the peasants, only the criterion of size counted.

The coffee beans left on the sieve were then emptied into the second wooden container. It was a slow and tedious job, this grading of the coffee, but it had to be done. After one's coffee had been painstakingly graded, it was carefully put in sacks and weighed. Gaidon Lihimba knew that the weighing of the coffee was the most critical stage in the whole operation. So, he positioned himself strategically near the weighing scales to ensure that the clerk recorded the weights correctly. He had heard stories of some unscrupulous clerks tempering with the figures in order to swindle the peasants of their money!

"Hey, Mr. Chairman," said the clerk recording the weights,

"why do you stand so close to me, your shadow is falling on the page in the register, and I can't see clearly. Give me enough room, will you?"

"Don't mind my shadow. We can bring a hurricane lamp to give you more light, if you like."

"Oh, but a hurricane lamp will only make the air stuffy and hot."

"Well, then don't complain about my shadow."

"You seem to be eager to see the needle on the weighing machine, and the figure I am recording in the register. Do you think I'm trying to cheat?"

"That's your own supposition, not mine."

"Look here, Mr. Chairman, I've done this job for twenty years. I've bought coffee from villages which had thousands of tons of coffee, not a few bags like you have here. I've never cheated. Why should I cheat poor people like you?"

"My dear man, you are putting words in my mouth. I've never said you intend to cheat us. Why are you so sensitive about non-issues?"

"Gentlemen," interrupted Bakari Mchope, "if you people start arguing like that, some of us will never get that money to-day."

"Stop arguing and get on with the job. We want our money today," said Susa with a sense of finality.

"Alright gentlemen," replied the clerk, "if you want us to pay you your money today, leave us room to do our work."

Gaidon Lihimba was not to be moved. He remained exactly where he was, and the clerk reluctantly went on with the job. After all the coffee had been carefully weighed and the weights recorded, the head clerk informed the peasants that to-day's payment was what was known as "advance" payment. On a later date, they would be paid arrears which would depend upon the price the coffee would fetch in overseas markets. This piece of information was music in the peasants' ears. They hadn't known about this. Old Bakari Mchope hadn't quite grasped the message, he asked Yeremia Kahongi who was standing near him, "What did he say? Will they pay us a second time?"

"Yes, that's what he said. They will pay us a second time."

"For the same coffee?"

"Yes. Apparently today they're paying us only part of what we should be getting."

"I think I'll ask Lihimba to clarify this point. Lihimba, can you clarify this point or can you ask the clerk to repeat what he said?"

Lihimba asked the head clerk to repeat what he had said with regard to the payment of arrears, and the clerk slowly gave the following explanation, "The Coffee Authority buys coffee from the peasants for the purpose of reselling it to overseas buyers and thus obtain foreign exchange which is greatly needed to buy many of the things the country needs, but which are made overseas. A tractor from England can not be bought by Kondowe money. We can only buy the tractor with their own money. Now, the only way for us to get their money is to sell them the things they want. These things include coffee, tobacco, tea, pyrethrum, cotton, sisal, cashew nuts, and so on. That's why the government, through the various Authorities which have been created to deal with the various cash crops, does everything to encourage the farmers to grow more and better quality cash crops.

"Now, when the Coffee Authority buys your coffee it often doesn't know in advance what the price of coffee is going to be in the overseas market. So, the Authority pays you an advance based on a fraction it hopes to realise in the overseas market. After the overseas buyers have bought the coffee, the Authority then knows how much money it has realised. It uses this money to meet its overheads and so on and the surplus is payed to the farmers in the form of arrears."

This explanation was received with applause and hand clapping. The Coffee Authority must be an excellent organisation, thought the villagers. It so happened that this being their maiden crop, much of the coffee did not qualify as grade one. So the people received less of the advance money than they had anticipated. But, by their standards, it was a considerable sum. The average earning of most households was fifteen thousand shillings. A few individuals like Susa, Chawanda, Kahongi and Lihimba managed to exceed the twenty thousand shillings mark. This was a real windfall for the village, and everyone vowed to work harder on his coffee *shamba* in order to improve the quality of the coffee so that the following year, it would all be graded number one.

A few days after the sale of their coffee, the villagers held one of their weekly meetings. Chairman Lihimba thought it wise to remind his village mates about the many good plans they had made to improve their village life before they squandered the money. But he soon discovered that it is much easier to get people to agree on schemes when they have no money in hand, than when they have money. For, when schemes are made with empty pockets what's being done is no more than building castles in the air, an easy feat to achieve. Thus, it had been all too easy for the Kindimba Juu peasants to talk about modern houses, lorries, shops and workshops, piped water when they had no money. Things were different now every one made his own plans, and they let the Chairman know this.

"Mr. Chairman," said a young man, of course we still remember those plans, but we did not say we should start implementing them immediately after we sold our first coffee."

"Yes, that's right," added another. "We never agreed to begin implementing the schemes so soon. By all means, let's keep our plans in mind, but for the time being we should allow people the freedom to spend their money the way they want. After all, aren't we going to get arrears? Why worry. We can begin working on our schemes afterwards when we've accumulated enough money!"

"That's precisely my point," said Chairman Lihimba. "The reason why I brought up this matter today was that there's always the tendency of thinking that if we want to accomplish great things, we have to wait until we have accumulated large sums of money. I happen to know what money is. I used to handle some in my youth in Lilungu. You see, the moment money comes into your hands, you always find ways of spending it, and it never accumulates! What I'm suggesting, therefore, is that we begin implementing some of our plans by putting aside a fixed amount of money for this purpose. So we may agree that each household puts aside three thousand shillings, then we would be sure that we were on our way towards meeting our objective. You see, a practical step, however small, is more important than big declarations of intent."

"That's all very well, Mr. Chairman," said another young man. "But look at most of us, look at our wives and children. We walk in rags. Our wives have no household utensils. Surely, it can't be wrong for us to buy our families and ourselves nice clothes and useful household things?"

"Oh, certainly," answered Chairman Lihimba. "I do hope that you're going to do something for your families. Don't misunderstand me. I'm not saying you should bury all the money you received the other day and wait for the day we begin implementing our plans! I'm saying that you should put aside some money for this purpose, and spend the rest wisely. I hate to see some of our children in tattered clothes, and some of our wives scantily dressed. We must think of all our dependants, especially our wives with whom we toil in the *shamba* from day to day. Use your money wisely, don't squander it on useless things."

At the end of this discussion, Lihimba's suggestion carried the day. It was agreed that each household should put aside three thousand shillings for use in implementing the plans to which the villagers had committed themselves. But Lihimba was careful to ensure that this was not a mere verbal promise. In the following few days, he proceeded to collect the money from every household. He then arranged with the mobile bank at Lusuma to visit Kindimba Juu, and all the family heads were made to open fixed bank accounts with the initial sum he had collected from them.

What happened in the ensuing months made Lihimba chuckle to himself, for it became clear to him that if he hadn't hurried up with his plan to make the villagers open bank accounts, there would have been no money left. Young men from his village journeyed to Lusuma and bought a lot of fancy things: tiny transistor radios some of which were worn on the necks like charms, coloured *vitenge* shirts with outsize sleeves, high heeled shoes popularly known as *raisoni*; bell bottoms, sun goggles, neckties, imitation wrist watches, and so on. A few bought second hand bicycles which they decorated with several mirrors and coloured ribbons. Some bought beds, mattresses, pillows, bed sheets and blankets. They also bought household utensils for their wives: plates, bowls, kettles, water buckets, and so on. Two unmarried young men got female partners at this time.

These women could not be regarded as wives in the proper sense of the word; for it was common among the indigenous Wahenga to elope with women during the coffee season when most young people had plenty of money. The women usually remained with their partners only long enough to help them exhaust their money, and then they ran away from them. The young Wampoto from Kindimba Juu took advantage of this practice among the Wahenga, and enticed two young Wahenga girls. At this time too, *Mzee* Susa was seen frequenting a number of Uhenga villages. Although he did not, in fact, get the two wives he had vowed to get, it is most probable that he had initiated moves towards that objective. Whatever the fate of *Mzee* Susa, life was changing fast for the Kindimba Juu villagers. Already their present situation was much better than it had been when they were in Yola.

In May of the following year, the villagers got the arrears promised them. They got more money than the advances they had received. Gaidon Lihimba did not forget to remind them about the bank accounts they had opened the previous year. This time the villagers willingly agreed to deposit twice as much as they had deposited the year before. In a few months time, that's to say, in September, they had more advances when they sold their coffee for the second time. This time each household had harvested coffee from one thousand trees or more. So they all got roughly twice as much money as they had the previous year. Indeed, money was now rolling in!

Gaidon Lihimba realized that it was not enough to keep reminding the villagers about the grand plans they had made for their village, he had to show the way by example for the others to emulate.

He persuaded his specially trusted friends, Yeremia Kahongi,

Chawanda, Charles Buka and his own young brother, Niklas, to begin making bricks. The idea was to make them work together as a team. They would first make enough bricks to build Gaidon's house, and then they would make more bricks for each of the others. These people knew how to make bricks since the white missionaries had taught them the art.

Without any further delay, they set to work. They located a hillock that had suitable clay for brick making. It took them two months to make enough bricks for Gaideon's house. The task of making bricks entailed making wooden frames for laying the bricks, digging up the clay, and most difficult of all, fetching enough water to moisten the clay so as to form a sticky dough of mud, packing the mud in the wooden frames, and laying the bricks. You should have seen Kahongi, Chawanda na Niklas at this time! They were covered with mud from head to toe and they were scantily dressed in sackcloth. It was hard work, but the five villagers were determined to see this work through.

After laying the bricks, there was the task of ensuring that the bricks did not crack while drying. This meant providing shade for the bricks by covering them with grass. After the bricks had dried, they were arranged in a kiln. Then followed the tedious task of collecting firewood to provide sufficient heat to bake the bricks. It took Gaidon and his friends three whole days working day and night, to fire the bricks and have them baked properly. It is important when burning bricks to ensure that the temperature in the furnace below the pyramid of bricks is not allowed to fall. This means that firewood must constantly be fed into the kiln.

All these things had been meticulously followed by Gaidon and his friends and after a week of waiting, when the red-hot bricks had cooled, the five villagers congratulated themselves when they saw the result of their labour, lovely looking red bricks.

While many of the other villagers were spending their money buying fancy things, Gaidon made arrangements with Lusuma merchants to provide him with building materials. He bought cement, corrugated iron sheets, window and door frames, glass panes and sanitary ware. He had all these materials stocked in his house. The following year, as soon as the rains were over, he started building his brick house. There was no problem getting a *fundi* to build the house, for there were many of these in Uhenga. So, six years after the Wampoto had settled in Kindimba Juu, Gaidon Lihimba had built for himself a big modern brick house which was the pride of the whole village. Party and government officials from Lusuma visited Kindimba Juu to see Gaidon's house. Indeed, here was an example to be followed not only by Kindimba Juu residents, but also by other villagers elsewhere in the Republic of Kondowe.

To the Kindimba Juu residents, Gaidon's house brought mixed feelings. While most of them generally felt proud that their Chairman possessed such a beautiful house, a few of them felt a sense of shame mixed with envy. Some recalled the way they had squandered their money on useless things; and others remembered Gaidon's advice, and they all vowed to follow his example by building brick houses as soon as possible. The possession of a brick house became the dream and ambition of every Kindimba Juu resident.

Gaidon's trusted friends Kahongi, Chawanda, Charles and Niklas had their houses ready two years later. Everybody else followed suit; and so, it was, that ten years after the founding of Kindimba Juu village, virtually every family had a durable brick house with a corrugated iron roof and a cement floor. It was in this tenth year of its existence that the village was judged the best in the whole of Lusuma Province, and from then on the village was given the new name of Mwongozo.

Eight

The year in which Kindimba Juu village changed its name to Mwongozo was an exceptionally wet year. Weather stations all over Kondowe recorded rainfall figures which were higher than those recorded in any other year in the past thirty years. The effect of this extraordinarily high rainfall was to cause excessive flooding of the rivers, and the areas most affected were those bordering Lake Nyanja. The numerous rivers descending down the Livingstone mountains burst their banks upon reaching the level plain of Unyanja and the water wandered at will over the villages. In the north, the great river Ruhuhu burst its banks and its waters inundated such villages as Nkaya, Njomoli, Mwera, and Ndumbi. In the south, rivers Munyamachi, Luholochi, Yungu, Mbawa, Lwika and Luekei also burst their banks and their waters did havoc to a string of villages along the lake shore.

As if the flooding of the rivers wasn't bad enough, the level of the lake also rose, partly due to the increased rainfall, but mainly due to the damming of river Sonje in Ushisha. To the southern tip of lake Nyanja in Ushisha is the mighty river Sonje which, under normal circumstances, acted like a regulator of the level of Lake

Nyanja, for it emptied the water of the lake into the ocean.

Three years ago however, the Ushisha government had completed its multi-purpose scheme which had involved the construction of a high dam across river Sonje at Chipoka. Studies carried out by the Ushisha government before launching the scheme had shown that the impounding of the waters of Sonje river would cause the inundation of only an insignificant area of land bordering the lake in Ushisha. Unfortunately, no consideration had been given to the effect the dam would have on the land in Kondowe! Now in this fourth year of its existence the artificial lake created by the dam at Chipoka reached its highest level, raising the water level of Lake Nyanja by a metre and a half. Indeed, Archdeacon Lamborne's prophecy thirty years ago was in danger of being fulfilled. A rise of the water of the lake by a few metres, he had said, was enough to obliterate over half of the land bordering the lake, the land known as Unyanja!

It was 5 a.m. on a February morning, and still raining as it had been doing, non-stop, during the last two days. The few villagers still left in Yola village were snugly asleep. There were fewer than a hundred families still left in the old village, for, since the historic departure of Gaidon Lihimba and his fellow pioneers ten years ago, a number of other Yola residents had followed and settled in what was now Mwongozo village. The few still left in Yola were quite satisfied with life, for having been able to appropriate more land for themselves they were able to produce enough food for themselves. Fish was also more plentiful now since fewer fishermen were left to plunder the lake.

Chairman Josaphat woke up from sleep imagining he had dreamt hearing the wailing voice of an old woman. He aroused his wife Rosalia from sleep. "I've had a bad dream," he told his wife. 'I heard somebody wailing in distress… Listen, here it comes again!" They both strained their ears to listen. Sure enough, there wafted into their dark room the unmistakable sound of running water and the wailing voice of an old woman.

"Please help, I'm drowning," said the voice outside.

"I think I can recognize the voice," said Josaphat. "It is Mama Susana."

"Wait, don't go out! This may be a witch," said his wife.

"Never mind your witches. I'll go and find out."

So saying Chairman Josaphat flung open the reed door of his house, and alas, water rushed into the house. A little distance from the house, he could see the silhouette of a person wading waist deep in water.

"Quick, light the hurricane lamp!" Josaphat called to his wife, while he himself plunged into the raging water to rescue the old woman. He reached Mama Susana, and holding her by the hand led her into the house. In the meantime, his wife Rosalia had lit the hurricane lamp. Both of them helped the old lady into a spare bed in the adjoining room, and Josephat left his wife to take care of her while he himself braved the rain and raging water again and disappeared in the backyard of his house where he collected sand and put it in a sack. He then placed the sack at the door of the house thus effectively preventing more water from rushing into the house. He entered the adjoining room to see how Mama Susana was doing. By then Rosalia had covered the old lady with her *kitenge*. Josaphat was unable to make out anything from the old woman's unintelligible words. It was clear to him that she was suffering from shock. There was nothing he could do at this hour of the morning except pray for the best and wait for daybreak.

Just as it was beginning to dawn, Josaphat went outside the

house to make a general survey of the situation. What he saw made his blood run cold. There was water as far as the eye could see. Some of the village huts had disappeared and most of the houses that were still standing were surrounded by water, so that individual families were virtually marooned. As hours passed, brave men from all parts of the village waded through the floods to chairman Josaphat's house in order to consult with him on what steps to take. Every one came with his own story of the catastrophe: there were those whose domestic animals had been swept away by the flood, and some who had lost everything except their lives. There were those who had spent the night on trees and on roof tops, and there were those who had swum several hundred yards to save their lives. Fortunately there was no news of anybody drowning. As the news unfolded, it became clear that the cause of the trouble was that both the Luholochi and Munyamachi rivers had burst their banks a kilometer or so from the village.

Unlike Gaidon Lihimba of Mwongozo village, Chairman Josaphat had no idea how best to deal with the situation. All he could venture to suggest was that the people should wait for the floods to abate and then move to higher ground near the foothills. He could not see farther than his nose. He could not see that the land near the foothills was too rocky to be suitable for human settlement. It was Sefu who pointed out the short sightedness of thinking about the foothills.

"How can any sensible person suggest we crowd ourselves on those rocky hills?" He asked. "Nothing can be grown there. I think if these floods don't subside, there's only one alternative for us – to migrate from here. We should not feel ashamed to follow our relatives in Mwongozo. They will welcome us, I've no doubt."

"Look here, gentlemen," said Pius Nyota, "before we go into

long term solutions to our problem, we must decide what we should do immediately! Right now we have people who are homeless. Some have lost everything. By evening today, some will have nothing to eat; and if the rain continues, we may have no house left standing in the village. We must find an immediate solution to our problem and leave the long-term question of migrating until later."

"Until later. When?" persisted Sefu. "I really think it's absolute nonsense to think of short term solutions. The only solution is to pack up and go. I've already made up my mind. This afternoon I'm packing all my belongings in my canoe and I'm leaving this damned village!"

"What, pack your things in a canoe?" asked Andrea Matutu. You mean you are moving to another village in Unyanja? Tell me, which one. If our village is flooded, it's most likely that other villages along the lake are also flooded. I thought you were talking of going to Mwongozo! But I know you can't go to Mwongozo and leave your big canoe and fishnets!"

"Where I go is none of your business. But I'm going away all the same," countered Sefu.

Borgias Mfanyaki, one of the very few able bodied young men left in the village, became indignant. He felt that his elders were wasting time quarrelling instead of making practical suggestions to solve their present problem.

"Gentlemen," he said, "I think what we should do immediately is notify the party and government about our plight. We should send a courier to Lusuma."

"I don't like the idea of calling government officials here," said 'king' Emilias. "We had famine here ten years ago and we were helped by government. If we call government again, they're sure going to force us to leave this village. Don't call government if we can help it!"

"I totally disagree with Emilias," said Evans Ndumbalo. "What's wrong with notifying the government? As a matter of fact, as good and loyal citizens we've got to inform the government. If it is discovered afterwards that we purposely decided not to inform the government about our problem, and if the floods get worse and lives are lost, we shall be held responsible, and then you will know what government is."

It was finally agreed to send Borgias Mfanyaki to Lusuma to inform the authorities about the floods. But due to counter arguments by Emilias and others, it was agreed that Mfanyaki should start off after two days. In the event of the floods abating, Mfanyaki would not have to go to Lusuma.

More frightening news came the following morning. Log canoes left on the beach were afloat in the lake. The level of the lake had risen, and extraordinarily high waves had devoured the sands of the beach!

All the men in the village rushed to the beach to save their canoes. In a few hours time, the waves became mountainous. They pounded the land with incredible force. The villagers helplessly watched their beach huts being washed away like toys. The canoes floated on the lake and in danger of being lost, so the fishermen pushed the little canoes as far inland as they could and left them in the cassava fields. But the waves continued to pound. In the morning of the third day, huge boabab and mango trees which had once stood several yards from the beach had been undermined by the waves and were now floating in the lake. The little canoes, which the fishermen thought they had saved, had either disappeared or they were floating far out on the lake! Indeed, the damming of river Sonje at Chipoka was having its full impact on the poor fishermen of Yola village! The notoriety of rivers Munyamachi and Luholochi was nothing compared with the vengeance of the lake. The prophecy of Archdeacon Lamborne was being fulfilled before the eyes of the villagers.

Panic stricken, the villagers in a body, ran to their village primary school, and Josaphat who had once been the head teacher of the school, but now the village chairman, led prayers which were intended to implore the Almighty to save them from the deluge.

As they were praying, some of the villagers wished Bakari Mchope was still among them. He might be able to arrest the onslaught of the waves! Unfortunately, Bakari Mchope was miles away in Mwongozo village, probably sipping black coffee in his newly completed brick house.

Just as the prayers were coming to an end there was a stampede as everybody rushed to the door of the little schoolroom now turned into a chapel. What had caused the stampede was a strange sound of something flying overhead. The fishermen had occasionally heard and seen airplanes flying over their village, but the sound they were hearing now was unlike that of an aeroplane. It appeared to them that whatever was flying over their village was so near to the ground that it was about to land; for the pole and mud school building shook a little causing bits of plaster on the walls to fall. Some of the villagers thought the school building was collapsing.

The strange sound of the flying object mingled with the booming sound of the waves and the torrential rain which had started falling again, made even the bravest among the villagers cower. As they streamed from the little room into the heavy downpour outside, they saw, in the direction of the lake, the blurred shape of a strange looking machine with a long tail and long propellers revolving on its topside. It was the first time most of these villagers were seeing a helicopter. Only Emilias had seen helicopters in South Africa. The helicopter was circling the village. When it came towards the school building, again some of the villagers bolted back into the room. A few brave ones remained outside in the rain waiting for the worst to happen.

The police helicopter was in fact searching for signs of life in order to rescue any marooned villagers. What had happened was that after they had agreed to send Borgias Mfanyaki to notify the authorities at Lusuma, he had slipped away that same afternoon without minding the foolish advice of people like Emilias that he should start off after two days. Borgias had walked the whole night and had reached Lusuma the following day. There he had delivered his important message to the KPP provincial Chairman and the Chairman had notified the provincial governor. He in turn had contacted police headquarters in Lilungu by telephone and Captain Mabruki and Sergeant Iddi Simba had been dispatched to Lusuma post-haste to carry out rescue operations. At Lusuma, the two policemen from headquarters had been joined by Corporal Msangi who was to guide them to the flood area.

Sgt. Iddi Simba who was carrying a pair of binoculars had spotted the few villagers outside the school building. Capt. Mabruki who was at the controls brought the helicopter directly above the school playground, and Cpl. Msangi who had a loud speaker called out:

"Don't be afraid. We've come to rescue you. Everybody, please, make your way to the school play ground if you can. If you can't, remain where you are, but stand in the open so we can see you. Carry no luggage with you, but you may bring your money. Enter the box at the end of the cable which we're lowering, three at a time! Old women, children and the disabled first! Don't be afraid…!"

Then Capt. Mabruki played a recording of the famous KPP song, *Pamberi na KPP*, forward with the Kondowe Peoples Party. As the familiar melodies filled the air, the villagers joined in the singing and clapped their hands. The rescue operation was on. The marooned villagers were taken to the upper part of Ngumbo village. When all of them had been brought to safety the police helicopter returned to Lusuma where it collected provisions for the rescued villagers. Late that same afternoon the helicopter was back, and it dropped a few bags of foodstuff for the rescued villagers.

It was not until several weeks had passed that the floods subsided and the lake level stabilised, and the villagers were able to return to their village of Yola. By then, only about half of the village area as it was before the flood, was habitable. Most of the villagers had to start life from scratch.

Nine

The National Executive Committee of KPP had directed that every province should review the villagelization programme to see if there were still people in the province who had not yet moved into permanent registered villages. If such people still existed, they had to be persuaded to join registered villages at once. Force, the NEC had warned, should be avoided as much as possible in moving the people, for the party did not want a repetition of the embarrassment it had felt fifteen years ago when the villagization programme had suffered disrepute due to the mistakes of some over zealous party officials.

It was Chairman Gaidon Lihimba of Mwongozo village who started it.

"Mr. Chairman," he told Mr. Malekano, the provincial Chairman of KPP during a meeting at Lusuma at which the NEC directive was being discussed. "We must admit that we in this province are lagging behind in the villagization programme. Other provinces have done much better. Here we still have too many people still clinging to the so-called traditional villages. Persuasion seems to have failed. I think a little arm-twisting won't be in bad taste!"

"It would be better if you were a little more specific, Mr. Lihimba," said the Chairman. "Which are the traditional villages you have in mind?"

"Of course you know them. Our Secretary here knows them. It's simply because we are afraid of using a little force that you pretend not to know these villages."

The Secretary that Lihimba was referring to was the Lusuma provincial governor. According to the Kondowe constitution, all provincial governors were also the Provincial Secretaries of the KPP. Following the directive of the NEC all provincial executive committees of KPP had to meet and discuss the implementation of the villagization programme. Chairman Gaidon Lihimba of Mwongozo village, Chairman Chengula of Ngumbo village, and a few other village chairmen happened to be members of the Lusuma Provincial Executive Committee of KPP:

"Mr. Chairman," said delegate Chengula from Ngumbo, "I thought we were supposed to be frank at these meetings, and not to hide our thoughts. Why doesn't Mr. Lihimba mention the villages he has in mind?"

"I'm surprised," retorted Lihimba, "to note that even my friend Chengula doesn't know the names of the villages next door to his own! If you're all afraid even to mention the villages by name, how do you expect to be able to exert pressure on these people? Now that you want me to tell you the obvious, I'll do so. The villages of Yola, my own birth place, Nindai, Nambingi, Malongo, Tawi, Ndonga, and a few others along the lake shore are no longer suitable for human settlement. People in these villages must be made to move away from them. Persuasion won't do. I know these people.'

"Mr. Chairman," "I fully agree with Mr. Lihimba. These people must be forced to abandon their villages and move to more productive areas. We have tried to persuade them, but our efforts have been fruitless," said the Secretary.

"Tell us, Mr. Chengula, why are these people stubborn?" asked the Chairman.

"Let me explain," answered Gaidon Lihimba, not letting Chengula have a chance. "It's not so much a matter of being stubborn. We Wampoto are not stubborn by nature. We are not as stubborn as the Wahenga, for instance. But it so happens that fishermen the world over develop such a close attachment to the sea and to fish, that it is almost impossible for them to imagine life away from the sea. You see, a fisherman's child likes to smell fish wherever he goes. When we were young, we used to leave the scales of *dagaa* on our hands even when we went to school. It was quite common for teachers to drive us to the lake to wash our hands before being allowed to sit in the classroom!"

The meeting roared with laughter at this revelation.

"Mr. Chairman," said Chengula, "I'm not amused. I can't sit here and listen to my fellow tribesman despising our tribe! Is he implying that this country should have no fishermen? Is fishing a useless occupation? Is it not possible for people to make a living out of fishing?"

Lihimba replied, "I'm not implying any of the things my friend is saying, and of course, I'm not despising my own tribe! It's precisely because I don't want my people to be despised that I want us to do everything in our power to help them, even if it means using a little coercion. I don't want my fellow tribesmen being left behind while others develop. Of course, I know that people can make a living out of fishing, but what kind of fishing? Certainly not the kind that's going on in those villages. That kind of fishing can only enable the fishermen eke out the barest minimum of existence. It cannot enable them to raise their standard of living. They will remain like that until 'kingdom come!'

Again the meeting roared with laugher.

"What do you mean by "kingdom come?" Do you wish our people to die?" asked Chengula.

"Please address the chair," retorted the Chairman. 'Those of us who know Mr. Lihimba well understand his great anxiety to uplift the lives of his fellow tribesmen. We know what he has being doing in Mwongozo. What he really means is that fishing alone is not enough to provide the necessities of modern life. With your primitive fishing gear and methods, you are simply unable to catch enough fish to make fishing a worthwhile economic activity. Fishing should be coupled with farming. But if you have no land, where do you grow the crops? It is true that the villages that Mr. Lihimba has mentioned have no land on which crops can be grown. Take the village of Tawi, for instance, what's there but rocks, rocks and more rocks?"

At the end of the day, the meeting resolved that the provincial Chairman of KPP should visit all the villages concerned and hold a *baraza* in each village for the express purpose of urging the villagers to move to registered villages.

This was done. In every village the chairman was listened to politely but nobody had any intention of leaving. The main argument advanced by the villagers at every *baraza* was that the people were happy and satisfied with their life as it was. To force them to abandon the villages was to interfere with one of the most basic of human freedoms, namely, the freedom of association, the freedom to live with those one chose to live with and to live where one chose. Much as the provincial KPP Chairman tried to explain that the party urged them to leave so that they might enjoy greater freedom from poverty and squalor, the villagers remained unimpressed.

A week after Mr. Malekano had completed his mission, representatives of the six villages, Yola, Nindai, Nambingi Malongo, Tawi and Ndonga met, at Nindai under the Chairmanship of Mr. Kagunila. Together they drafted a memorandum to the KPP provincial Chairman. This memorandum was meant to be an authoritative joint reply to the chairman's proposition that they abandon their villages and start life in new villages. It was a long and tortuous memorandum. The thrust of its argument was, again, a philosophical one; for, it challenged the party and government to define human happiness and human progress. It questioned the correctness of equating progress with the possession of material things; and it reminded the party about one of its basic tenets which was belief in basic human rights and freedoms. It ended by reiterating once again that the villagers were happy as they were. There was no need to make them happier!

The provincial Chairman did not like the audacity with which the memorandum had been written. He consulted the provincial governor about it, and the latter suggested that the only way now was to use government machinery to enforce the issue. But after more discussion and bearing in mind the NEC warning not to use force, they decided to seek the advice of the National Executive Committee itself.

So the memorandum from the villagers was forwarded to the Chairman of the NEC who was none other than the National Chairman of KPP himself. In a covering letter, the Lusuma provincial chairman described the efforts he had made to knock sense into the heads of the villagers; he gave a graphic description of the geographical, social and economic position of the six villages;

and he cited Yola village as the village which had been ravaged by red locusts many years ago, and which had recently been reduced to half of its original size due to the floods. He ended the covering letter with a plea for speedy action by the NEC.

The NEC, true to its principle of fair play, wrote back to the Lusuma provincial chairman asking him to notify the villagers concerned that the NEC was sending a delegation to the villages to assess the situation, hear the villagers' views, and then make recommendations to the National Executive Committee.

The NEC delegation led by the Hon. Jonston Makaburi, member of parliament for the central province, consisted of three other people: Rev. Israel Lilanika, Abdu Omari, and Justice Hezron Mwaipyana. At Lusuma, they were joined by Mr. Malekano, the provincial KPP Chairman. The previous week word had already been given to the villages about the forthcoming visit of the NEC delegation and it had been agreed that all the villagers should assemble at Yola to meet the delegation. In the meantime, the leaders of the villages went round urging people to ensure that they attend the big *baraza* on the appointed day. It was important, said the leaders, that the NEC delegation should get the impression that the villagers were happy and contented with their life. Everyone was urged to put on his or her best clothes for the occasion. This was going to be a greater occasion than any Sunday or feastday they had known. Housewives were urged to prepare lots and lots of *ugali* and rice to feed the guests. Three goats were to be slaughtered, and most important of all, there was going to be a display of various foodstuffs on the day of the *baraza* in order to show the guests that the villagers did not lack food. School children were urged to wash their uniforms and to ensure that they looked smart and happy on that day. The main intention was to impress the delegation.

A day before the delegation arrived, six sacks full of dried small fish, two baskets full of delicious looking smoked fish, two sacks of rice, several baskets of cassava flour and of groundnuts were stocked at the primary school where the baraza was to be held. Chairman Josaphat had gone round the other five villages to collect the foodstuffs. Nor was this all. A few days earlier, he had sent people as far afield as Mwongozo village to buy pumpkins, bunches of bananas and cabbages. All these were to be put on display on the great day!

The great day arrived. It was a bright May day. The lake was calm and blue. One could never believe that this lake now looking so placid could at times assume the shape of an angry monster. White swans were now resting on the lake as if they were floating dead bodies. Cassian Malolela, the enterprising village school teacher, had prepared his pupils well. They had rehearsed and rehearsed the reception ceremony. A number of songs in praise of the party and its leadership, and the struggle of the proletariat had been mastered to perfection, and four particularly bright kids had memorized many lines of *ngonjera*.

As the morning wore on, villagers from the five other villages began to trickle into Yola village. Eventually they streamed in by their hundreds, and filled the school play ground. Chairman Lihimba of Mwongozo village who had known about this important meeting, also came along to watch the proceedings as an observer. Some of the Yola residents who saw him did not like his presence.

The ladies came dressed in brightly colored *khanga* and *vitenge*. Most of them had exceptionally huge headdresses popularly known as *totoro*. As a matter of fact, in some instances, full-length *vitenge* were used as headdresses. The men had fished from their boxes or pots the best of their *vitenge* shirts, in most cases those displaying the symbol of KPP on the chest, and having extraordinarily wide sleeves.

At 11.a.m. sharp, the delegation arrived, and it was accorded a tumultuous greeting of ululations and hand clapping. Two young boys of the *chipukizi* group stepped forward smartly and placed scarves on the necks of the distinguished guests. This was immediately followed by a well-rehearsed song of welcome sung by the school children. After the guests had been shown to their seats, *ngonjera* was recited. The *ngonjera* was a touching piece of poetry, which expressed the villagers' unflinching loyalty to the party and government, and their hope that the KPP as the father of the oppressed would see to it that they were not molested or treated like inanimate objects. It pointed out the fact that the lake shore villages did not lack anything that contributed to human happiness. God had given them the lake, which provided then with delicious fish; and he had given them land, which though sandy; produced enough cassava, rice, groundnuts, pumpkins and cabbages to keep the people nourished!

After each stanza the men clapped their hands and the women made ululating sounds. Chairman Josaphat felt a little uneasy, however, for he noticed that none of the guests was clapping hands as the *ngonjera* progressed. The guests appeared to be showing only stony politeness.

The proceedings of the *baraza* began as soon as Mwalimu Malolela had signaled to his pupils to sit down orderly in a corner of the playground. The provincial KPP Chairman, without the customary greeting consisting of a litany of political slogans, plunged straight into an outline of the history that had led to today's meeting. He touched on the party's policy of villagization and described the efforts the Lusuma province had made in establishing permanent villages. He talked about the decision taken by the provincial executive committee, which had led to his visit to the six villages some time ago, and he went on to mention the villagers' memorandum which had prompted the NEC to send today's delegation.

After this brief introduction Mr. Kagunila from Nindai who had been chosen as the spokesman of the villagers, asked if it was in order for him at that juncture to read to the audience a statement prepared by the villagers.

"Does the statement contain anything different from what's covered by the memorandum you sent to the provincial Chairman?" asked the Hon. Johnston Makaburi.

"No, Sir. The statement simply reiterates what we've said in that memorandum," answered Kagunila.

"If that's the case then there's no need to read it out. The villagers know what the statement says, since it is their statement; and we know what you've said in your memorandum, which, as you say, is not different from what's in the statement. You may however, submit your statement to us and we'll look at it later."

This was the first rebuff for the villagers and the second for Josaphat: first the guests showed mug faces during the *ngonjera* recital, and now they don't even want to hear the villagers' statement! Kagunila looked at his fellow villagers as if he was asking for assistance, but none was forthcoming. He walked a few paces forward and handed the piece of paper he was holding to Mr. Makaburi.

"What we're really interested in at this meeting," continued Mr. Makaburi, "is to find out for ourselves what your situation here is really like. We shall ask you some questions, and we shall listen to what you have to say. But don't forget that we also have eyes. We shall attach more importance to what we're told. Perhaps you could begin by telling us what your main economic activity here is?"

"Fishing, of course," answered Kagunila.

"How much fish do you catch in a year?" continued Justice Mwaipyana.

"A lot of it. Over there we've six bags of dried small fish for you to see. That represents only two nights' fishing. How much do you think we can catch in a year?" asked Kagunila.

"Well, don't ask us. Tell us how much you catch in a year!" retorted Justice Mwaipyana.

"How much money does a fisherman earn in a year by selling fish?" asked Mr. Abdu Omari. "Give me a rough figure."

At this juncture, a man in the audience was heard sneezing violently, and all eyes turned to look at him. It was Gaidon Lihimba. He raised his finger, and Mr. Malekano who was chairing the meeting allowed him to speak.

"Sir, if people living along the lake shore were making three thousand shillings a year, I'd not have migrated to Mwongozo!"

"But, sir," shouted Josaphat, standing up, "how can you allow people from upcountry villages to spoil our meeting? The man who has just spoken does not belong to any of the six villages represented here."

Mr. Makaburi leaned towards Malekano to ask who the intruder was, and Malekano whispered in his ear that that was Gaidon Lihimba, the man who had been Chairman of Yola village before he started Mwongozo village which was now the best village in the province. He told him more about Lihimba. Mr. Makaburi, looking in the direction Lihimba was sitting, and not looking at Josaphat, replied, "This is an open *baraza*. It is sometimes good to get advice from outsiders who may be able to look at issues objectively. Besides, I'm informed that the gentleman who spoke was at one time Chairman of…"

"Sir, now we know that the delegation is prejudiced against us," blurted Kagunila. "First you refuse to listen to our statement, and now you want outsiders to influence the meeting!"

"This delegation is not prejudiced for or against anybody," said Mr. Makaburi. "Be calm and answer our questions."

"Apart from fishing, what other economic activities do you have?" asked Rev. Israel Lilanika.

"We grow cassava, rice, groundnuts, pumpkins, bananas, cabbages and other things, and we sell some of the foodstuff. You can see samples of these things over there."

"Where do you sell the produce? Who buys them?"

"People."

"Which people?"

"Those who happen to pass by."

"Do you have a market here?"

"No. We sell our food in our own homes."

"I see."

Gaidon Lihimba coughed aloud thus drawing the Chairman's attention, and Mr. Malekano allowed him to speak.

"Sir," he said, "I hope that at the end of the meeting you'll be able to see some of the gardens where the pumpkins, bananas and cabbages are grown!"

"Oh, yes, we shall be delighted to see these gardens," said Mr. Makaburi. "As a matter of fact, we'd like to see them right now. While the meeting is going on, one of us will go and have a look at the gardens. Could one of you take him there, please?"

Rev. Israel Lilanika left the meeting accompanied by Chairman Josaphat who was to show him round. They headed in the direction of Josaphat's house. When they reached the house, Josaphat invited the guest to sit down briefly while he fetched him a bowl of *togwa*[2] from the house. He came back with the bowl of *togwa* and immediately fell on his knees.

"Please, sir, listen to what I've to say. I implore you, on behalf of my people, to have pity on us. We're poor fishermen, and we have an attachment to the lake, which other people cannot understand. Our people cannot imagine life without fish, without canoes, and without the lake. For this reason we were foolish enough to try to deceive you into believing that we grow all those things we've put on display today. The truth is that we don't grow any pumpkins, cabbages or bananas here. Formerly we used to grow some bananas but the banana groves have all been washed away into the lake. We collected these things in order to ensure that you were persuaded to leave us here. I'm prepared to give you personally a sack of dried small fish if you could only tell your colleagues that you've seen the gardens, alright."

"Before you do that, tell me first where you got the cabbages, and bananas from?"

"We bought them from Mwongozo village the other day."

"Foolish guys. So you thought you could fool us so easily?"

"Had it not been for Lihimba, we might have fooled you," lamented Josaphat.

"No, you wouldn't have. We've seen that kind of trick before. There was an instance when some villagers had placed five hundred heads of cabbage bought from a market in a newly cultivated garden! When we visited the garden it had just been watered and, boy, it really looked like an excellent cabbage garden! As we were leaving the garden, I happened to stumble on one of the cabbages, and to my surprise the cabbage came off its moorings on the wet soil.! We tried to lift the others, and they all came off the ground easily. You know what we did then? We forced the village Chairman to pluck out all the five hundred cabbages and carry them on his head from the garden to his house, which was a mile away!"

'What're you going to do with us now?'

'The worst part of the whole thing is when you suggested bribing me with a sack of dried small fish! I could send you to court for that, and hopefully get you to do a two year stretch!'

"Please don't say that."

"Let's go back to the meeting."

When Rev. Lilanika and Chairman Josaphat returned to the meeting, the villagers knew that the worst part of the meeting was coming, for they knew that their foolish trick had been uncovered. As soom as Lilanika had joined his colleagues he whispered to Mr. Makaburi about his findings. Mr. Makaburi burst out laughing. The Chairman called the meeting to order and asked Rev. Lilanika to address the meeting. Rev. Lilanika then spoke with relish about the non-existent vegetable gardens. He challenged anyone in the audience to tell the delegation if he knew of a place in any of the other villages where vegetable gardens could be viewed, but no one dared say anything. Only Gaidon Lihimba was heard chuckling to himself at his seat.

In closing the meeting, Mr. Makaburi reminded the audience once again that his Commission's duty was simply to submit its recommendation to the NEC. It would be the NEC itself, which would reach the final decision on the fate of the villages.

---

[2] *togwa* = sweet, non-alcoholic drink

Ten

Inspector Christopharus Baraka had picked his people carefully from among the crack Field Force Unit. Sergeant Laurent Kilindo was his number two on this mission. Sergeant Kilindo entered the first armoured landrover together with five other men from the riot squad. Inspector Baraka himself entered the second armoured landrover with five other men. The twelve men, all dressed in combat uniform and iron helmets were armed to the teeth with semi-automatic rifles, tear gas and clubs. Both Inspector Baraka and Sergeanr Kilindo carried walkie-talkies, and radio antenae could be seen on both landrovers.

It took them just under one and a half-hours to descend the treacherous Livingstone mountains to lake Nyanja. Now they were heading northward to the six notorious villages whose residents had flouted an order by the National Executive Committee.

Johnston Makaburi's commission had strongly recommended to the NEC that the six villages along the lake be abandoned forthwith, since the residents there were eking out only the barest kind of existence. The NEC had agreed with this recommendation, and through normal channels, the residents of the six villages had been served with an order to leave the villages. In fact, they had been given a deadline date by which they were expected to have left the villages. But the deadline had gone by and the villagers had not stirred. On their part, the villagers thought they were playing a game with the party and government to see who between them would persist the longest in their demand. They hoped that by persisting in their refusal to abandon the villages the party and government would simply give the game up and forget the whole thing. Little did they know how seriously the party and government had taken the villagers' stubborn behaviour!

The twelve-men expeditionary force reached Malongo village, the southern-most of the six villages at 5 a.m. when it was still dark, and none of the villagers was up and about. Sergeant Kilindo and his five men alighted from their armoured vehicle. Inspector Baraka's vehicle proceeded along the dirt road to Yola. It came to a stop outside Chairman Josaphat's house. It was 5.30 a.m. The five men alighted from the vehicle, ready to take orders from the inspector. Josaphat was aroused from sleep because of the movement outside. He opened the reed door of his house, only to face the grim reality outside.

"Sergeant Kilindo, Sergeant, Kilindo!" called Inspector Baraka in his walkie-talkie, "Do you hear me? Over!"

"Sergeant. Kilindo here. I hear you. Over!"

"Group arrived safely. Mission to start immediately. Over."

"Yes, mission to start immediately. We're ready. Over."

"Ensure no spilling of blood. Repeat, no spilling of blood. But raze houses to ground. Over."

"Yes, will ensure no spilling of blood. Houses to be burnt. Over."

Josaphat, who was trembling as he watched the grim faced

askaris checking their rifles, tried to give the KPP salute, but nobody seemed to notice it.

"You're the owner of this house?" asked Inspector Baraka.

"Yes, sir."

"Good. You have exactly ten minutes to remove your belongings and put them in a safe place outside the house. After ten minutes we set the house on fire. Understand?"

"But, sir, how can you…"

"Stop arguing, you old skunk," said a young *askari* clubbing Josaphat in the region of the belly. As he was clutching his belly and retreating into the house, his wife Rosalia emerged and met him at the door.

"What's happening?" she asked.

"Don't ask questions. Do as they say. Come in and let's remove our belongings."

They both disappeared into the house and began removing their household effects: bedsteads, a wooden box, pots and pans, baskets.

While this was going on it occurred to Muggy, Josaphat's faithful terrier, that no one, including FFU *askaris* had the right to disturb her master's peace at this early hour of the morning. She came out of the house barking her head off and menacingly advancing towards Inspector Baraka. One of the boys squeezed the trigger of his SAR putting a clean hole in Muggy's head, silencing her forever. Pussy, the black furred cat, was much wiser. When she saw what had happened to Muggy she silently slipped into the nearby bush, never to be seen by Josaphat and his wife again.

The report of the gun had awakened people in most of the houses in Yola. A gun? Who could be firing a gun in Yola? Nobody was known to possess a gun. As the villagers were still puzzling over the question of the gun, they saw fire belching from Chairman Josaphat's house.

"Josaphat's house is on fire!" shouted one old man.

"Let's go and assist him," said another.

"But how about the gun? First we hear the report of a gun, and now we see Josephat's house on fire. Something must be going wrong," said yet another.

They did not have to go and assist Josaphat. They would soon be having plenty of work to do! As the two old men were still talking, two *askaris* appeared. By now the six *askaris* had divided themselves into three groups of two; each group going its own direction and ordering the villagers to remove their household things before they set fire to the houses. There were screams of despair all over the village as house after house was put ablaze. The *askaris* made sure that nothing remained in the village which resembled shelter of any sort. Even the primary school building was razed to the ground. By mid-morning, Yola village lay in ashes.

"Sergeant Kilindo, Sergeant Kilindo! Do you hear me? Over."

"Sergeant Kilindo, speaking. I hear you, alright. Over."

"Mission accomplished at Yola. Over."

"Mission accomplished at Malongo. Over."

"We're ready to move to Nindai. Over."

"Meet you at Tawi, 2 p.m. Over."

"Will ensure we're at Tawi at 2 p.m. Over."

At 2 p.m that afternoon, the twelve-men expeditionary force converged at the tiny village of Tawi. It took them only one hour to set the whole village ablaze. At 5 p.m. they moved to the nearby Ndonga village and burnt down everything resembling shelter. By sun set Inspector Baraka and his little force of eleven men were enjoying the cool breeze of the lake shore at Ndonga. Casting their eyes northward along the lake shore areas, they could see only smoke.

"Where are the poor chaps spending the night?" asked Private Mathias.

"That's none of our business," answered private Amos.

"I suppose there're no wild animals in these parts?"

"How do I know?"

"By the way, Amos, did you notice some of the girls in Nindai village? Boy, weren't they beautiful?"

"Why don't you go back and spend the night there?"

"Who, me? No, sir. They'd murder me if I was seen there alone. After what we did to them!"

"But you could explain that we were only obeying orders, and that in reality our hearts were bleeding for them!"

"True, my heart was bleeding for them. I won't be able to sleep to-night. I'll have nightmares."

"Oh, come on, that's not the language of an *askari*."

"You know, Amos, the worst part of it was when we burnt the food barns. Some had not removed all their foodstuff when we set the barns on fire."

"You're telling me! I discovered at Tawi village, after I'd set fire to four of the beach huts, that there were fishnets in them. It was too late to remove them. So they all got burnt! Most of them were nylon nets, so it was only a matter of minutes before they became ashes. You should have seen one of the old men whose nets had become ashes. I thought he was going to faint."

"Good Lord, you burnt the nets! You see, for these people a fishnet represents the most valuable thing among their worldly possessions. Losing a net means losing the only means of livelihood."

"I know."

"Who was it who said something about man's inhumanity to man? I remember reading something like this somewhere."

"Ah, but ours was not inhumanity. We were obeying orders. After all, the ultimate objective, the real intention, is to help these people attain a better life."

"What? Attain a better life after they've lost their nets? How'd you imagine they're going to attain that life?"

"Well, they've to start all over again, I suppose!"

"How?"

"That, I'm afraid, is their *shauri*. You know, Mathias, our leaders often teach that if you want to cure a boil, you've got to use surgery, not aspirin."

"And so you think we've been doing surgical work today?"

"Yeah, why not?"

"I suppose you're right. This then is a question of the end justifying the means?"

"What d'you mean. Can't follow your reasoning."

"You've said, haven't you, that since the intention is to help these people attain a better life, the use of harsh methods like burning their houses is justified."

"Of course, yes. By the way, who did you say spoke about man's inhumanity to man?"

"I forget who the bloke was. But I'm sure I read it in one of the literature books we used to read at school."

"So, you read literature at school?"

"Yeah, I did a bit of it."

"And with all your learning you end up burning people's houses?"

"I think I'll quit the force as soon as I get back. After the bloody job we did today I won't be happy in the force any more."

"Conscientious objector?"

"I suppose you could put it that way."

"Come on, don't be faint-hearted. Be a man!"

The exhausted *askaris* had their supper by the lakeside. It consisted of tinned beef, tinned fruit and biscuits. After they had had their meal, they entered their armoured landrover and returned to base in Lusuma.

* * *

Evans Ndumbalo put more wood in the fire. His three young children and his wife were fast asleep on a mat a few feet away. Josaphat was sitting beside him near the log fire. His family was also asleep on a mat nearby. The two men looked at one another without saying a word. There was no need for words, for each knew what was going on in the mind of the other. Ndumbalo's eyes watered a little but he fought back the tears. He was one of the few sad cases where the *askaris* had unwittingly burnt the food barn before he had time to remove the foodstuff.

Having no shelter left, the villagers had collected themselves in groups of two or three families to spend the night under the starry sky. At every group a log fire was kept burning throughtout the night to keep wild animals at bay. Mats were spread out near the fire and while children and their mothers slept, the men stayed awake to keep watch. At each group domestic animals could be seen tied to posts nearby, and the household effects carefully arranged on one side.

Josaphat broke the silence of the night. "Is it worth calling a meeting tomorrow?"

"What for?"

"To discuss our situation."

"Nonsense."

"Why nonsense?"

"Cause there's nothing to discuss. When you're dead, you're dead. What do you discuss? We're dead people. To burn a person's house is to kill him."

"Don't you think some people might need advice on where to go from here?"

"Everyone must be knowing where he wants to go."

"Maybe we should meet at least to bid farewell to our ancestors."

"What do you mean?"

"I mean what I'm saying; bid farewell to the dead. We've buried our people here. We must conduct a brief ceremony of *tambiko*."[3]

"Maybe you've a point there. Why don't you call everybody for the ceremony tomorrow?"

"Yes, I think I'd better do that, first thing tomorrow morning."

At this juncture, the still night air was pierced by the sharp shriek of a leopard. Had private Mathias known this, he needn't have wondered as he did, whether there were wild animals in these parts! Leopard's most favorite food is the flesh of goats and dogs. In this particular night, the goats were tied to posts near log fires all over the village. The dogs were also lying in the open, close to their masters. They were thus prey for the marauding leopards.

The two men took up their spears and clubs which they placed by their sides in anticipation of this kind of eventuality. They strained their ears to find out which direction the sound came from.

There, it came again, loud and clear. The leopard couldn't be more than a few hundred metres away. But leopards are cunning creatures. They move quietly and stealthily before suddenly springing on their prey. Josaphat and Evans waited. Then they saw some of the goats beginning to get nervous, and Evan's dog began to make a low growl, the sign of fear. That was it, thought Josaphat and Evans. The big cat must have arrived. But then it was quiet again. The goats calmed down and Evans' dog curled its tail and lay down snugly near the fire. But the two men were not to be deceived. They knew this to be part of the cunning strategy leopards use when stalking their prey. They lie low in the direction towards which the wind blows, so the goats or whatever else they may be hunting can't smell them.

So, with steel nerves, the two men waited, spear in one hand and club in the other. If only they had a powerful torch they'd be able to scan the surrounding area. But as it was, the log fire only accentuated the darkness around them. Then, suddenly, at a time when the goats were least expecting danger, there was a thud! The goats panicked as they tried to break away from the posts to which they were securely fastened. Evans and Josaphat bravely charged forward. There was just enough light to enable them to see the silhouette of the big cat struggling with a goat. The leopard would have dragged the goat into the nearby bush had it not been fastened to the post.

Evans Ndumbalo threw his spear with all the strength he could summon. But due to the poor light, the spear could not be aimed at the right spot on the leopard's body. It pierced one of the hind legs, tearing a tendon. Now, leopards are usually shy animals, if you make enough noise, you can scare one away. But an injured leopard is something else. It is the deadliest animal in Africa, deadlier than a lion! It will fight, and die fighting!

By the time Ndumbalo's spear tore the leopard's tendon, the leopard had already started sucking the goat's blood. So Ndumbalo's spear had not only caused pain to the big cat, it had also interrupted its meal. It left the bleeding goat lying on the ground and with the speed of lighting sprang at Ndumbalo's neck. Evans Ndumbalo defended himself with his club. But the leopard's claws tore his right hand inflicting nasty wounds. Josaphat came along, and using both hands he thrust his spear through the leopard's ribs with such force that the spear came out on the other side. This sent the animal wriggling on the ground with the spear sticking from its sides.

A lesser animal would have succumbed to death due to the blade of steel that had cut through its body. Not a leopard! It sprang up, claws fully unsheathed and teeth ready to dip into anything, and advanced towards its attacker. Josaphat stepped aside momentarily; but Evans, now seething with anger because of the pain in his arm came forward with his club. Aiming the club at the leopard's head he pounded it more than ten times, until he was sure the carnivore was completely dead.

The battle with the leopard had awakened the wives and children. They screamed and cried, but there was nothing they could do, not even run away. Josaphat called to the women and children to remain near the fire and not to run away into the dark. The children and their mothers were horrified to see Evans Ndumbalo's injured arm,, but the gallant Ndumbalo cheered them all up. After Josaphat had applied first aid to Ndumbalo's arm using local herbs, he proceeded to skin the goat that had been slain by the leopard.

At daybreak, as most of the villagers were preparing to leave, each family going to a destination of its choice, Josaphat went round the various places where the families had spent the night and invited the heads of families to meet briefly at what used to be his house.

By 8 a.m. all the elders were gathered at Josaphat's place. Josaphat then introduced the subject of bidding farewell to the ancestors. The proposal was unanimously accepted, and they all left immediately for the nearby graveyard.

The oldest among them was Mzee Yimuha. He went to the graveyard carrying a hen and a knife. They all stood round the grave of Nungwila who was reputed to have been the founder of the village of Yola. Taking the knife from his pocket, Mzee Yimuha quickly severed the head of the hen and let the blood drop onto the grave, then he buried the carcass in the same grave.

After this simple ritual he said, "You, our ancestors, children, friends and relatives who lie here, we've come to bid you farewell. Circumstances force us to abandon this village which you bequeathed to us. We know not where we're going, and what fate awaits us. But two things we promise you: wherever we may go, we shall return here once each year to pay you homage; and if any of us dies, we shall bring his body to be buried here among you."

"So be it," responded the others.

Having made this solemn promise, Yimuha took a little soil from Nungwila's grave and cast it in the air. Then he knelt beside the grave and kissed one of the tombstones. One by one, the others followed suit and kissed the tombstone.

Just as they were beginning to leave the graveyard, they saw two figures approaching. Presently, the two men joined the group of elders at the grave yard. They were Gaidon Lihimba from Mwongozo village and Borgias Mfanyaki.

"Comrades," Lihimba said, 'I come to you as your brother. I come to offer you a brotherly hand of assistance in your hour of need. Borgias has told us what happened here yesterday, and indeed my own eyes have seen the devastation that has taken place. I've come to ask you all to come along with me to Mwongozo. There's plenty of land there for us all. There's no…"

"But who told you that we needed your assistance?" asked Josaphat, interrupting Gaidon Lihimba.

"I don't have to be asked for assistance by my own kith and kin. I know you need assistance, and it's my moral duty to offer it, if I can."

"And you Borgias, who told you to go to Mwongozo to ask for assistance?" Josaphat asked.

"Nobody. As soon as my house had been burnt down I left for Mwongozo. I knew if I didn't, many of our people would be misled by silly people like you."

"How dare you call me silly!"

"Because had it not been for you, many of us wouldn't have remained here after the locust famine and after the floods. You are the one who objected to people moving to Mwongozo; and your leadership has been the least effective."

"Gentlemen," said Evans Ndumbalo, nursing his badly wounded arm, "there's no time for quarrelling. My arm's hurting. I want to go to a place where I can take a rest. It's really only a matter of individual choice. Those who want to accompany Gaidon to Mwongozo should be free to do so, and those who want to go elsewhere may do so. I myself will follow Gaidon Lihimba."

"So will I," said Pius Nyota.

"And me, too," said Mzee Yimuha.

"Gentlemen," said 'king' Emilias, "don't be over hasty about this. Think of our nets and our…"

"Shut up!" said Borgias Mfanyaki. "You may go to hell with your nets! You are the people who've been responsible for keeping us backward. Always thinking about nets, fish, canoes. We've had these things for years, and what are we now? Just as poor as we've always been!"

"There's one more thing I wanted to say," Gaidon Lihimba said, stepping between Borgias and Emilias. "Do not hesitate to follow me because of your nets. Bring them along with you."

"Are you crazy? What are we going to do with nets up there?" asked Emilias.

"You see, in Mwongozo village, we live according to plans. Our present plan is to make a road linking Mwongozo and the lakeshore. We already have a village lorry. Our aim is to enable those who want to come here to fish, to do so easily. As a matter of fact, we intend to organize ourselves in such a way that each day a group will come down here to fish. So you see, if you bring your nets with you, you will be able to have the best of both worlds."

This piece of information pleased them so much that they answered in unison, "if that's the case, we'll come along with you!"

Only Josaphat, Emilias and three others did not want to follow Gaidon Lihimba. These five obstinate people left the graveyard and headed towards their former homes to collect their families. To Gaidon Lihimba this was indeed a sad parting of the ways. He was, however, satisfied that the majority of the elders were ready to start off immediately and follow him to Mwongozo.

[3] *tambiko* = a peace offering to the dead

Eleven

Namatui village is situated approximately twelve miles to the south of what was once Yola village, and three miles inland from the lake. Formerly this place was known as Namatui Mission, but with the introduction of the villagization programme, the 'village' aspect of Namatui had become more prominent than its 'Mission' aspect, and it had become more fashionable to speak of Namatui Village rather than Namatui Mission. Rev. Kleofas Malyunga, the Father-in-charge of the mission station became the priest-in-charge after the death of Father Wolfgang. Now he had become a less prominent figure than Mr. Saburi, the Village Chairman.

It had taken the little group of people from Yola a whole day to travel from Yola to Namatui. They reached Namatui in the evening. Josaphat, Emilias and the three other elders and their families made up a party of twenty people. The women were carrying heavy luggage on their heads, while the men were carrying young children on their shoulders as well as driving their goats in front of them. Movement was thus rendered extremely slow, especially since from time to time, they stopped by the river side to prepare food and eat; and at times the goats ran astray in pursuit of fresh pasture.

Their first problem was where to find accommodation for the night. Memory of the battle with the leopard was still fresh in Josaphat's mind. Moreover, the area around Namatui village being one of dense jungle, quite unlike the open country to the north, where villages like Nambingi, Nindai and Yola had once stood, was most likely to be infested with lions!

Josaphat's fears increased as the shadows of sunset appeared. He asked his people to remain outside the first house they came to in Namatui, while he himself set off to find the village Chairman. A young boy offered to take him to Mr. Saburi's home.

The Chairman, a short gentleman in his late fifties, and showing signs of obesity and a balding head, was seated outside his house playing a game of *nchuwa* with three other gentlemen. *Nchuwa* is a game, which is similar, but not identical, with the *bao*, commonly played by townsfolk in Kondowe. *Nchuwas* has slightly different rules, and it uses forty-eight holes instead of thirty two as in *bao*. Chairman Saburi and his friends had toiled the whole day in the village communal farm and now they were relaxing by poring over *nchuwa*.

"Zee! Zee! Zee! Zee! Paa… na! Waa!" Chairman Saburi, though in a state of great mental concentration, seemed to be thoroughly enjoying himself as he juggled the pebbles from hole to hole.

"Sir," said the young boy who had escorted Josaphat, "this gentleman wants to see you."

"Zee! Zee! Zee! Zee!" continued the two competing sides

without any of them looking up at the boy.

"Sir, this gentleman wants to see you!" shouted the boy almost kissing the Chairman's ear.

"I'll skin you alive if these people 'kill us," barked Saburi looking up at the boy and the man standing by his side.

Now, in the language used in the game of *nchuwa,* when a side loses a game, that's to say, when all its pebbles have been taken or 'eaten' by the opposing side, then the defeated side is said to have been killed!

That's why Saburi threatened to skin the lad alive if, due to his interruption, Saburi should lose the game.

"What's it?" he asked looking at the lad as you would look at a fly that had entered your glass of beer.

"This gentleman…"

"Alright, wait until we finish this game," continued Mr. Saburi.

"Zee! Zee! Paa … na!"

It was not until Saburi's opponents had been vanquished, until Saburi had scooped all the pebbles from the opponent's twenty four holes while his own side had a few pebbles still left in some of the holes, that he looked up.

"Mputa," he crowed, looking at his opponents, "don't challenge me to *nchuwa* again. You're a novice at this game. I used to play *nchuwa* with the late Kadewele."

"You come to my house tomorrow," said Mputa. "I'll try again then. I'm not used to playing with these kinds of pebbles, and I'm not used to playing on the ground. My *nchuwa* is carved on a board like *bao,* and I use smooth round seeds, not rough pebbles like yours."

"Lame excuses! Alright, I'll meet you on your home ground tomorrow," said Saburi confidently.

"Now then, what about this gentleman?" Saburi asked turning to look at Josaphat.

"What's your name?" he asked.

"My name's Josaphat. We have just moved away from Yola village."

"We? How many are you?"

"Twenty, sir. I mean we are a group of five families: ten adults and ten children."

"You are the stubborn ones who wanted to play games with the government, eh?"

"Well, not quite that. It was a matter of ignorance."

"We heard what happened to your villages. Matter of fact, others from the villages that were burnt also arrived here yesterday. Where are your people?"

"At our house," answered the young boy.

"You go and bring your people to the Mission building over there. Do you see that building over there?" Saburi asked, pointing to a red brick building.

"Yes."

"Alright. Hurry up. I'll go and speak to Father Malyunga. You'll find me at that building."

"Thank you."

Josaphat and the boy returned to the boy's home, and Josaphat told his people to follow him to the Mission building as directed by Mr. Saburi. The building to which the homeless fishermen were directed was, in fact, one of the dormitories of Wolfgang Trade School, built in honour of the late Father Wolfgang, at Namatui Mission. The boys who normally occupied the building were on holiday just now, and at the request of the village Chairman, Father Malyunga had kindly agreed to give temporary accommodation to the homeless fishermen who had arrived the previous day.

Chairman Saburi saw Father Malyunga soon after parting with Josaphat, and informed him about the latest influx of homeless fishermen from Yola. Father Malyunga agreed that these too be accommodated at the Wolfgang Trade School where they could stay for a few days while the village government sorted out their problem by allocating them residential plots.

When the weary villagers from Yola arrived at the Trade School, their hearts were cheered a little to see people from Nambingi, Malongo and Nindai who had arrived there the previous day. In all, there were forty families which added up to two hundred individuals.

Father Malyunga beaming benevolently, welcomed the newcomers to Wolfgang Trade School and assured them that the church appreciated their plight and therefore he was ready to give them whatever assistance he could give. They would be allowed to remain at the trade school for two weeks during which he hoped they would be able to prepare temporary homes for themselves. During the two weeks they were camping at the school, the church would help them with daily rations of cassava, flour and beans.

Chairman Saburi then announced to the newcomers that the following morning all the heads of families should assemble in a hall nearby to meet the village government.

At 9a.m. the following morning, one of the church bells began to toll. At first the newcomers thought some kind of church service was about to begin but, no, this bell was not heralding a church service, but a meeting of the village government! In spite of Bishop Makita's protestations, Father Malyunga had immersed himself so much in the affairs of the village government, that he had allowed the use of the church bell to announce village government meetings, and he had put the parish hall at the disposal of the village government. All meetings of the village government and standing committees were held in the parish hall. Father Malyunga himself was treasurer of the village as well as the custodian of the village shop. The poor homeless fishermen who had never known what an organized village government was like were ebout to have their first taste of one!

The Namatui village government consisted of Chairman Saburi, a Secretary, a Treasurer, in the person of Father Malyunga, a Manager, an Agricultural Officer, a Health Officer, an Engineer, a Cultural Officer, and two other members, who were as it were, ministers without portfolio. These ten people constituted what you might call the cabinet, or the executive wing of the government. But the highest body of the government, the highest legislative body, was the village Council which consisted of all the village residents aged eighteen and above.

The government discharged its duties principally through its five standing committees: the Finance and Planning Committee, the Defence Committee, the Agricultural and Economic Affairs Committee, the Transport Committee, and the Cultural and Social

Affairs Committee. It was a complicated set up.

As the homeless fishermen filed into the parish hall they noticed a number of young men in baggy khaki uniforms carrying clubs. They were later to learn that these were members of the village militia, who on occasions like this, acted as bodyguards to ensure that the sessions went smoothly.

Mr. Kagunila from Nindai, not knowing the demands of protocol on such occasions, entered the hall wearing his tattered felt hat and sat down. The next thing he saw was a club descending on his right shoulder!

"Remove that dirty rag from your head!" whispered a militiaman, reaching out his left hand to remove the felt hat.

"I'm sorry, I didn't know we had to remove hats," answered Kagunila. "But must you use your club for that?"

"You will know a lot of things here." said the young militia. "Next time I'll aim the club at your head!"

The Chairman entered the hall followed by the other members of the cabinet. A militiaman gave a signal to the forty newcomers to stand up. They remained standing until the Chairman and the other members of the village government had taken their seats, and then the militiaman waved for everybody to sit down. This was very much unlike the informal noisy meetings the newcomers had known in their old villages. Today, Mr. Saburi looked every inch the Chairman of his village. Immaculately dressed in a white *kanzu,* a black jacket, and embroidered *barghashia* and high quality leather sandals, he looked a totally different person from the man who was seen stooping over *nchuwa* the previous evening.

"Gentlemen," said the Chairman, "the purpose of today's

meeting is to formally welcome to our village, the people you see here and their families. These, as you no doubt know, are the people whose villages were destroyed by government in order to force them to move to registered villages. The party and government have been encouraging people to move into registered villages for some years now. Unfortunately, we have in this country people who never heed the advice of the party. The party is then forced to direct the government to use unpalatable methods to make them heed its advice. Perhaps this is no time for me to go through all this again. I do hope that these people have learnt their lesson. We are however glad that they've chosen to join our village. We certainly welcome them here and we hope that they will fully cooperate with us in our efforts to improve life in this village. I now call upon the village secretary to brief the newcomers about the set up of the village government and its committees. Mr. Secretary!"

The secretary stood up and gave an outline of the village government and its various committees. While doing so, he also introduced the Chairmen of the committees who were, in fact, members of the cabinet.

The various committee chairmen then took turns to describe in detail what their committees did for the village. The village manager followed, describing the weekly routine in the village. He said that there was a definite timetable of activities for each week, and that a rota of work was drawn up each week. It was the responsibility of each villager to know what job he was scheduled to do.

To the newcomers who had not been used to this kind of

life, all this was as bewildering as it was frightening.

Finally it was left to the chairman of the Agricultural and Economic Affairs Committee to tell the newcomers that they would be allocated one acre plots on which to build their new homes, and also four acres on which to grow crops. The allocation of plots would commence the following day.

As the newcomers were returning to their camp at Wolfgang Trade school, they were filled with mixed feelings. Some looked forward with excitement to the challenges of starting life in a new place, but others were not so sure if that was the kind of life they wanted to lead.

"You may as well forget about your *ngoma* 'kingship' Emilias," whispered Josaphat as they were walking back to the camp.

"I think I'm going to sell my drums to the school here. There doesn't seem to be any chance of playing *mganda* here," observed Emilias.

"Did you hear about the weekly rota?"

"What did that mean?"

"It meant that each week you will be told what to do. One week you may be required to milk the cows; another week to go fishing; another week to guard the village communal *shamba* against wild pigs and monkeys, and so on, and so forth."

"Really?"

"Yes."

"No freedom?"

"How do you mean, no freedom? Isn't that freedom?"

"I mean can't we be left to take care of ourselves?"

"Apparently, not. Well, I suppose there will be days when

we'll be left on our own, to work on our own *shambas*." "How about our wives? Will they also be ordered to to this and that like us?"

"Why not? Didn't you hear the other man talking about baby sitting, and cooking communal meals? He said that on days when we work on the communal farm, in order to enable the women to participate fully, some of them will be required to do baby sitting. Some of them will cook communal meals to be sent to the people working in the communal farm. So, you see, one day your wife or my wife will be baby sitting and another day they will be cooking meals for the rest of the villagers!"

"What is baby sitting?"

"Presumably the toddlers will be herded into one place, and the women chosen will stay with the toddlers, cook for them and possibly feed the smaller ones."

"But, what do they get by organizing life this way?"

"You're asking me? How do I know? Perhaps they become happier, this way. We have to wait and see."

"Happier? Look at their children. Look at the people we meet. They don't look any happier than we are. I bet we were happier in Yola than these people are. They are all in tattered clothes; and most of their houses are only grass huts. Our houses, which the *manjolinjoli*[4] burnt, were much better than these huts."

"But you forget that these are only temporary dwelling places."

"Aa, but some of the huts look old. They must've been built at least five years ago. I bet they will remain temporary dwelling places forever."

"I guess you're right. It seems that once they had put up these temporary huts, they got stuck with them, and now they have no way of improving them.'

"By the way, how much money did they say they got this year by selling crops from the communal farm?"

"I think the chairman said ten thousand."

"Ten thousand shillings?"

"Yes."

"I see. It looks like a lot of money. But how many people are here?"

"There must be at least one thousand of them."

"How much does each get if they share the ten thousand equally?"

"Ten shillings."

"Ten shillings a year?"

"Yes. But it doesn't mean that it's the only money they get. They have other ways of getting money, I guess."

"Which ways?"

"I don't know. Maybe fishing, or selling crops from their own shambas, or making articles for sale."

"When do they get the time to do these other things, with the village time table so tight?"

"Here comes the priest in-charge. We don't want him to overhear us."

---

[4] *manjolinjoli*: policemen (word used derisively)

Twelve

The task of allocating plots began promptly the next day. First, a list of the newcomers was drawn up, showing the heads of families and their dependents. Every male of the age of eighteen years and above was given a plot on which to build his house. Members of the people's militia measured the plots using ropes and pegs. The newcomers were instructed to ensure that the rows of houses were straight. They were warned that if a house was found to be out of line with the rest in a row, that house would be pulled down.

It took two days to complete the task of measuring the one-acre plots. Then followed the task of allocating plots on which the newcomers could grow crops. To the newcomers' dismay, they discovered that the plots allocated to them were not less than six miles from the village. The plots nearer the village had already been taken up a long time ago by those who had arrived first to start the village around the old mission.

Accompanied by members of the militia, all the male newcomers aged eighteen and above walked for a good two hours before they reached the bush which they were to tame into productive *shambas*. On the way to the bush they passed a five hundred-acre farm which was the village communal farm. Then they passed through *shamba* plots belonging to individual peasants. On arrival at the edge of the cultivated area, the task of measuring the four-acre plots began. It was hard walking through the thick jungle, but the indefatigable members of the militia, ropes and pegs in hand, did the job cheerfully.

"Josaphat," said Emilias as they were walking back from the bush after being shown their shamba plots, "have you ever seen a person growing shorter as he grows older?"

"No, not yet. But I guess I know what you're driving at."

"I bet we'll be shorter by several inches after a few years! Walking twelve miles to and from the *shamba* each day will no doubt wear away our soles and our general height will be reduced. Failing this, the legs will simply sink into the hips and bring about the same result!"

"Apart from the distance, did you notice that the soil in the area given to us is very poor?"

"I did, yes. It's very stony."

"Never mind. We can still grow cassava even in that stony soil."

"But how is cassava going to help us? We used to grow cassava back home, and now they bring us here only to grow cassava again?"

"Who are they? No one brought you here. You chose to come here!"

"Yes, but had they not burnt my house I wouldn't have come here."

"I say, Emilias, did you also notice the monkeys?"

"Yes, I did."

"I bet it's going to be one hell of a life trying to keep those monkeys from the *shambas.* Its alright keeping wild pigs at bay, but monkey's! There's nothing you can do to keep them away except by constantly being there and driving them away when they enter the *shamba."*

"But how can you drive them away when you're six miles away?"

"I suppose we will have to take turns guarding our crops during the day. Fortunately, monkeys don't feed during the night. They sleep."

"How about wild pigs?"

"Well, we'll have to erect a fence round the *shambas.* There's no way out."

"We can't do that this year, can we?"

"We have to build our houses and prepare our *shambas,* you know. We simply won't have the time to erect fences."

"I'm afraid we may not reap anything this first year."

The following three months were busy months for the newcomers. In two weeks, they had erected temporary huts using bamboo, sticks, ropes, grass and mud. They left Wolfgang Trade School dormitory and moved into their newly completed huts. Then they started collecting materials for erecting the permanent houses, a task which involved cutting poles and bamboo and preparing other building materials, and took several weeks to complete. After this, the actual task of building the houses began. In three months time the new comers had built themselves modest pole and mud houses similar to those belonging to the other villagers.

As soon as they started preparing their *shambas* the problem of distance began to be felt. They had to wake up at 5a.m. each morning in order to get to the field and start work before the sun got too hot. By the time they reached the field, they were already tired. At mid-day they would rest to take food. Work would be resumed at 2 p.m., but by 4 p.m. they would start off in order to reach the village before 6 p.m. The journey home in the evening left them dog tired, especially since they had toiled hard during the day. Indeed, so acute was this problem that some of the villagers decided to erect yet more temporary huts in their fields, usually on trees, as a precaution against wild animals, in order that they could be near their fields. This meant that male members of each family took turns to live in the field, thus not only cutting down on the amount of time used for walking to and from the fields, but also enabling them to guard their crops against wild pigs during the night.

But this arrangement, plausible as it was, had one big disadvantage. The poor wives of the newcomers often found themselves alone in the village at night. Rumour had it that some of the village officials, including Chairman Saburi, were often seen in the houses of the newcomers at awkward hours of the night, on the pretext that they were informing the newcomers about important forthcoming village events!

Meanwhile, the village government decided that the newcomers had had enough time to settle down, and that now it was time they were fully involved in the life of the community. The active village manager promptly began to include the male newcomers in the weekly rota: Some were to milk the village cows; others to guard the communal farm against monkeys during the day and wild pigs during the night; others were to go fishing, and so on. To the newcomers unused to this kind of life, this was gross interference in their personal freedom. There was nothing they could do but put up with the situation.

While doing the various chores, there were frequent interruptions necessitated by frequent meetings. No week ever went by without some kind of meeting being held: now to discuss the reception of some party or government official who was about to visit the village; now to discuss arrangements for celebrating a national day; now to simply meet and talk since the party bosses had always said that it was important that villagers should meet even if they had nothing to discuss, that the mere fact of sitting together was useful!

What bothered the newcomers most was that they were called upon to do so many things, that they had hardly any time left to do things of their own choice. In some cases, projects were started but never completed. Every committee Chairman had a project in mind, which he urged the villagers to undertake because it was important for the development of the village. For instance, the Chairman of the Cultural and Social Affairs Committee thought it was important that they should make bricks in order to extend the primary school building on a self-help basis. A fine idea. The villagers promptly started laying the bricks, but before they had made half the number of the bricks required, the village manager announced that everybody had to take part in digging a trench that would be used for laying the village water pipe. The health officer also agreed that the laying of the water pipe was of utmost importance to the village as it would ensure that the villagers had clean water which was essential for good health. So the laying of the bricks was stopped and the digging of the trench started.

After months of toil digging the trench, it was discovered that the pipes promised to the village by Lusuma, had in fact, not been ordered from Lilungu. So, the trench was abandoned and very soon it was filled in by soil and other debris and overgrown with bush.

The Agricultural Officer having just returned from a seminar at Lusuma at which the Provincial Agricultural Officer had urged everybody to redouble efforts in urging people to cultivate more food crops as the country was threatened by famine, announced that every square inch of available land in the residential area had to be planted with some kind of food crop. It was a matter of life and death, he said. So, every villager planted maize, cassava, beans, sweet potatoes, and vegetables on every available space outside his house, in addition to his big *shamba*.

But the health officer noted an increase in the incidence of malaria. He surmised that it was due to the growth of plants too near the houses. He made his discovery known to the village government, and the villagers were urged to keep their surroundings clean by clearing all the bush near the houses. But how about the food crops? Well, the village government allowed the villagers to retain their crops until they could harvest them: but in future, they were not to replant the plots close to their houses. The health officer had convinced the village government that it was the plants outside the homes, which were harbouring the mosquitoes and which were responsible for the spread of malaria.

The Agricultural and Economic Affairs Committee greatly valued the six dairy cattle the village had received from Lusuma for the purpose of propagating the breed in the Unyanja area. However, on the occasion of the Farmer's Day, the celebration committee that was a sub-committee of the Cultural and Social Affairs Committee decided that one of the dairy cows had to be slaughtered to feed the villagers as part of the day's celebration. A hot dispute ensued between the Agricultural and Economic Affairs Committee on one hand, and the cultural and Social Affairs Committee on the other. In the end, a vote was cast and the cultural and Social Affairs Committee won. So, one of the dairy cows was promptly slaughtered!

The many contradictions in the affairs of the village left the newcomers completely confused. Josaphat and Emilias were visibly annoyed by the way things were going in the village. They decided they would leave Namatui and follow their kith and kin in Mwongozo village. But first they would sound Lihimba by writing him a letter.

"Dear Gaidon,

We would like you to regard this letter as a sincere expression of our present predicament. After you've read what we have to say, we would like you to forgive us, your brethren, even if it may not be possible for you to forget the past.

You remember very well that we have opposed you at every turn. When you first suggested that we should migrate to what was then Kindimba Juu and now Mwongozo, it was I, Josaphat, who vigorously opposed you, but I also influenced the others to be against you. My friend Emilias who is here with me now, being no wiser than myself thought of nothing else but his **mganda** *'kingship'. More recently when our village became the victim of both natural and man made disaster, you did not cease to extend a brotherly hand of assistance. But the two of us stubbornly refused to follow you to Mwongozo.*

We have now learnt through bitter experience, the folly of our ignorance. We have discovered that there is a world of difference between moving into a new settlement with deliberate plans in mind as you did when you moved into Mwongozo, and being forced out of your village because you have nowhere to live.

In your case, you had all the time you needed to do things orderly. In fact, it took you nearly two years to complete the process of moving to Mwongozo. Our departure from Yola was traumatic. We found ourselves uprooted and cast into another community overnight. Our lives had to be, and they continue to be, planned for us by others!

The idea of living in the so-called development villages is undoubtedly a sound one. But our experience here reveals a number of short-comings in the villagization programme. First, the villages should not be allowed to have more than two hundred and fifty families. In the case of Namatui Village, there were already three hundred and twenty families when we arrived. We were twenty families altogether; so you can imagine a village of three hundred and twenty families, nearly one thousand six hundred people!

*As a result of the large population, the village **shambas** have to be located far away from the village, especially for those who, like ourselves, joined the village late. Our own **shambas** are six miles from the village. You can imagine what this means in terms of time wasted in walking to and **from the shambas**.*

*Second, related to the problem of our **shambas**, is another one of a social nature. We won't go into it in this letter, but briefly, it appears that some of the village officials have been taking advantage of our absence from home. It is rumoured that some of them have been seen in our homes at awkward times of the night! More on this matter when we meet you.*

Third, the thing that we find most intolerable here is lack of personal freedom. Life is so regimented out here that there is hardly any freedom left for us to do what we want. We are either at some meeting or doing something according to the village time-table. Now, we know that even you in Mwongozo have certain set routines, but we understand that you leave much more time to individual initiative than is the case here. At any rate, you do not have as many committees as we have here. It is these committees which stifle our freedom; for each committee feels it has to initiate some activity for us to engage in. Very often the committees give contradictory advice to us, thus leaving us utterly confused.

*When the **manjolinjoli** burnt our houses, they said that they did so in order that we should migrate to development villages where we would be happier. The NEC commission, which visited us at Yola also said the same. Well, all we can tell you now is that we are definitely far from being happy here, let alone being happier! It is our belief, in fact, our conviction, that it is wrong to manipulate human beings the way we are being manipulated here for, even if material progress could be achieved through these methods, and we doubt if it will ever be achieved yet people would never be happy. To us, happiness is closely tied up with individual freedom.*

We have therefore decided to join you if you will accept us. We are ready to move to Mwongozo anytime you decide to take us in.

We are confident that you will forgive us for our past misdeeds.
Yours affectionately,
Josaphat and Emilias

* * *

It was a day of great rejoicing when Josaphat, Emilias and the other three families from Namatui joined their kith and kin in Mwongozo Village. Mzee Susa, as Chairman of the welcoming party, proudly introduced the new arrivals to his newly married wife, a teenage girl of the Wahenga tribe.

Among the people welcoming the new arrivals was Jonathan Matupila from Ngumbo village. Josaphat and his friends were to learn later that Matupila had joined Mwongozo village a few months earlier, after his wife Lucresia had eloped with Mzee Mahinya.

The end.

GLOSSARY

Askaris : Soldiers, guides or policemen/women
Bao : (Swahili for 'board') is a mancala game played in swahili and Bajuu communities in Eastern Africa eg Zanzibar, Coastal Tanzania, Kenya and the Comores.
Baraza : A congregation or meeting.
Barghashia : A short rounded cap worn by Muslim men.
Bin : Son of a particular person eg Asha bin Juma
Boma : A settlement village which is designed for protection of cattles from predators and other tribes ; circular, fenced–in area made from logs used for keeping cows and goats ; surrounding central pen for cows and goats.
Chipukizi : An up coming group
Dagaa : A type of small fish
Donge : Money
Fundi : A person doing a specialised job by proffession
Jumbe : Head of town or street
Kande : A Tanzanian staple food of beans and maize possible with additional flavouring of vegetables and meat.
Kanzu : A long white robe worn by Muslim men.
Khanga : A traditional East African piece of clothing, rectangular in shape and is made from cotton. It is brightly coloured and printed in bold designs. It is purchased in a pair and it contains educational and informational words. It can be used in carrying children at the back, worn as skirts, scarves or over other clothes. It is purchased in pair.
Kitenge : Traditional East African piece of clothing, rectangular in shape and is made from cotton. It is brightly coloured and printed in bold designs but thicker than khangas. It is purchased in a pair.
Makopa : Sun drying of cassava, bananas or potatoes ; a type of flour produced as a result of peeling cassava roots, then left to dry under the sun to golden brown. Afterwords, they are

stacked and covered with banana leaves and left to ferment for two to three days until moulds appear , then they are sun dried. This process is common along the Coast and Southeast regions.

Nganda : A dance played by some residents from Dar es Salaam and Pwani.

Mwinga : A tree that grows wood which is used for furniture and other activities.

Myombo : A thin tree with small leaves that grows around dry parks.

Mzee : A person who has lived for many years ; a person who is highly respected.

Ngoma : A traditional dance or resulting from a traditional African drum musical instrument sounded by striking with sticks or hands made of a hollow round wooden frame with skin or parchment stretched tightly accros the open ends.

Ngonjera : Poetic dialogue which uses question and answers.

Pombe : An alcoholic drink.

Raison : High heeled shoes.

Shamba : An area of cultivated ground ; a plot of land ; a small farm.

Shauri : An opinion

Tunguli : Instrument used by witch doctors to store or preserve medicine.

Ugali : A thick mixture of corn and water, the flour is mixed and boiled in water. Ugali can be eaten with vegetables or with stew.

Uji : Porridge.